IN PLAIN
SIGHT

IN PLAIN SIGHT

MIKE **KNOWLES**

ECW Press

Published by ECW Press
2120 Queen Street East, Suite 200, Toronto, Ontario, Canada M4E 1E2
416.694.3348 / info@ecwpress.com

LIBRARY AND ARCHIVES CANADA CATALOGUING IN PUBLICATION

Knowles, Mike
In plain sight / Mike Knowles.

ISBN 978-1-55022-948-6

I. Title.

PS8621.N6715 2010   C813'.6   C2010-901259-3

Cover and Text Design: Tania Craan
Cover Image © Peeter Viisimaa
Typesetting: Mary Bowness
Production: Troy Cunningham
Printing: Solisco - Tri-Graphic   1   2   3   4   5

Mixed Sources
Product group from well-managed
forests, controlled sources and
recycled wood or fiber
www.fsc.org Cert no. SW-COC-001352
© 1996 Forest Stewardship Council

The publication of *In Plain Sight* has been generously supported by the Canada
Council for the Arts which last year invested $20.1 million in writing and
publishing throughout Canada, by the Ontario Arts Council, by the
Government of Ontario through Ontario Book Publishing Tax Credit,
by the OMDC Book Fund, an initiative of the Ontario Media
Development Corporation, and by the Government of Canada through
the Canada Book Fund.

Canada Council   Conseil des Arts   **Canada**   ONTARIO ARTS COUNCIL
for the Arts   du Canada   CONSEIL DES ARTS DE L'ONTARIO

PRINTED AND BOUND IN CANADA

ECW PRESS
ecwpress.com

For Andrea.
It could be for no one else.

CHAPTER ONE

The beeping woke me up. It was a steady drone, pounding out beat after beat. It was my heart I heard being digitally reproduced for an audience. The machine beside the bed was monitoring its uniform spasms. I lay with my eyes closed, ignoring the beeps, focusing on the other sound that erupted intermittently. I waited for what felt like ten minutes until the eruption happened again. A wet phlegmy cough started low in someone's gut and fought gravity all the way up. In the midst of the coughing fit, I opened my eyes and looked around the room. A second later, I closed them and tried to re-create the scene in my mind while the coughing subsided. The room was white, as were the machine and the bed rails. Handcuffs joined my wrist to the bed. The chair by the door was overflowing with a lot of bad suit. The fabric was worn and out of style. Every pocket on the jacket brimmed with papers and the tops of pens. There was also an angular bulge on the right side of the coat, visible under the thinning material. The suit and the gun bulge had cop written all over it.

Almost 4,000 beeps later, the cop got up from the chair. He had to take a few seconds to get his wind back from the exercise.

"Don't go anywhere," he chuckled.

The door creaked twice, open then closed, and my eyes opened. I was in a windowless box of a room. Fluorescent lighting showed every imperfection on the walls and the floor. Every scuff and scratch stood out and showed the age of the hospital room. I breathed deep and felt the air rush into my nostrils. The antiseptic scent made me nauseous. The sudden pang of discomfort tuned me in to every other pain I was feeling. A wash of anguish rolled over me. My head ached and my ribs hurt. I tried to reach up to my face, but the shackles held me solid. The chains slammed against the bed frame with a loud metal-on-plastic crack. The sound was an explosion in the small white room. I lay back and closed my eyes — expecting company, but no one came in.

I opened my eyes again and stared at the ceiling thinking back to the last thing I could remember. I had been forced to work a job for a mob boss. I had told Paolo Donati that I was done being his problem solver, but no one quit on Paolo. He used my friends to force me into finding who had kidnapped his nephews. I became a fixer again and found out that Paolo's nephews were kidnapped as part of a coup. His former right hand, Julian, wanted the brass ring and thought going after the boss's nephews would unhinge Paolo enough to knock him off his throne. The two mob heavies were on a collision course with me in the middle. I did the only thing that would keep me above ground. I led Paolo into his enemies' web and let nature take its course — after I got Julian admitting on tape that he killed the two kids. The info was enough to keep Julian away from me forever: the kids had powerful relatives in the States who would be honour bound to settle up with Julian if they found out what he did. I remembered walking away from Domenica's, Julian's restaurant, a free man. Then I remembered leaving the pavement. Everything after that was blank.

I took the alone time in the hospital room to research. There was nothing nearby that I could get my hands on, nothing to use against the cuffs holding me down. Everything I could touch was flimsy and soft. I kept looking for an option until I heard the doorknob twist. The door swung in, and the wheezing cop wedged himself back into his chair. I fake slept to the tune of beeping and coughing with crinkling plastic on drums. The cop ate at a rapid pace, pausing only to unwrap the snack on deck. It was as though he thought someone might burst through the door and take the food right out of his mouth. After about a minute, my nose picked up the scent of stale cigarettes. The cop was a smoker and enough of an addict to leave his post to sneak a smoke break. I tried to run through scenarios in which I could get my hands on the cop and out of the cuffs, but my arms had barely enough slack to reach the thin mattress. My lack of options took my hands out of my equations. My feet were free, but there was no guarantee that I could kick the cop in a way that would still leave me access to his keys or his gun. I couldn't lift his piece or pick his pockets with my toes anyway, so I let the idea drift out of my mind. I had to play the waiting game until a new opportunity presented itself.

I lay chained to the bed for two days feigning unconsciousness. Every time the fat cop took off to sneak a cigarette, I stretched out as best I could and looked for anything I overlooked before that would help me escape. I was always disappointed.

On the third day, I was counting the perforations in the

3

ceiling tiles with my eyes when the door opened earlier than I expected it to. I usually had a few minutes and a few hundred beeps before I had to begin faking sleep again. I quickly adapted to the schedule change and resumed my conscious coma, listening for the cop's breathing. What I got was something entirely different. Rubber-soled shoes squeaked as someone approached the bed. It wasn't the doctors or nurses — their footwear didn't make a sound. The fat cop had worn-in dress shoes that slipped on the glossy floor. I had heard him stumble and break his fall on expensive medical equipment several times. This was someone new.

The fluorescent light dimmed outside my eyelids as the person who was now standing over me took a huge deep breath and slowly let it out. This was not like the fat cop's breathing — this person was in shape. The breath lasted over thirty seconds. I took a slow breath of my own to slow my own heart. I didn't want the monitor giving anything away. Just as I finished exhaling, a heavy hand closed over my nose and mouth. The hand pressed down and the bed groaned in response. The machine beside the bed monitoring my heart picked up speed, but my body stayed slack. The beeping quickened its pace, becoming more and more of a solid sound as another hand tore the monitor pad from my chest. The machine registered a flat-line. It was going on too long. I could no longer afford to play dead. My mouth opened and found part of the hand over my lips. I bit down hard and tasted blood.

"Shit!"

The hand moved away as the door flung open. The fat cop rushed in, at his snail's pace, ahead of a nurse and a doctor.

"Morrison!" the fat cop said.

"Don't worry, Miller. Our patient woke up. It's a mira-

4

cle." The man who had been suffocating me was pressing his thumb over where I had bit. His face was to the door, giving me only a look at his suit; it was tight, but not like the fat cop's. The material was taut across muscular shoulders and arms.

"But the nurse's station got an alert that his heart stopped. Whatever was monitoring his vitals said he was dying."

"When you left for your little break, our patient must have removed the sensor. The alert wouldn't have happened if you managed to stay at your post."

"Sir, I . . ."

"Shut the fuck up, Miller. Get everyone out of here. I'll deal with you later."

"Now hold on a minute, I have to check on my patient."

"Later, Doc, later. Right now he has to check in with me. When I got what I want from him, you can have him."

"I am his physician, and while he is in this hospital he is under my care. Hospital protocol demands I check on him after an alert," the doctor protested. He had a hard time realizing that he was outranked on his own turf.

"Miller, get them out of here now!"

The fat cop turned and spread his arms. The pudgy net swept up the nurse and the doctor, both of whom obviously wanted no contact with the sweat-stained blazer, and forced them out of the room. The man over me slammed the door behind them before crossing the floor and unplugging the heart monitor. He dragged the fat cop's chair to the bed and sat down. He didn't say anything right away. He was too busy pressing an old tissue from his pocket onto the bite on his hand.

"You broke the skin."

"You tried to kill me."

"Nah, it was reverse CPR. It always works on fake coma victims."

"What if the coma was real?"

"Reverse CPR's got only one side effect I know of."

"Where am I?"

"Hospital."

"Who am I?"

"Cut the shit."

"Who am I?"

"I said, cut the shit." The cop stood, and I got my first good look at him. He was tall, maybe six-three, and muscular, not bodybuilder muscle but wrestler muscle. His body conveyed a sort of all-over strength. Not the kind that came from lifting a dumbbell over and over again, but rather the power that evolved out of years of driving people off their feet and then grinding them into the ground. His skin was dark, not black, more of a deep tan. It wasn't the olive complexion of the Mediterranean I was used to; the features were more foreign, the nose wide and flat and the forehead large. I had not seen this look before. The dark hair on his head was trimmed short. It was strong healthy hair; the kind that held its shape without gel. This cop was a tough bastard. It radiated off him. I could sense it like dogs sense other dangerous canines. He leaned in over me and outstretched his hand again.

"I know who I am. I want to know who *you* think I am," I said. My words stopped the hand from covering my mouth again.

"You're a guy who's in a world of shit. Way I see it, I don't know your name, but I know you're a killer. We found you in the road in front of that wop front, Domenica's. You had a gun on you, a knife, and a dog bone. There was something that looked like a tape recorder, but it got mashed to bits when the car hit you.

Funny part is, the restaurant was closed. There were three cars out front: one registered to the owner of the place, the second to a very bad man — one outside my department and paygrade. The owners of the first two cars weren't around, but the owner of the third vehicle, a van, was there. He was dead in the passenger seat. Caucasian, long hair, beard, name Gary Ford. Most people called him Gonzo though. Seems Gonzo was at the hospital earlier for a *fall*."

"Must have been some fall to have killed him."

"Nah, he walked out of the hospital with a clean bill of health. Well, he didn't walk so much as limp. The emerg Doc said the wound looked like a gunshot through the foot. Bullet went right through, so there was nothing to recover, but the impact drove some of his old canvas Chuck Taylor Converse into his foot. Into the . . . metatarsal bones, the doctor called them. Gonzo swore up and down that he stepped on a pickaxe in his garage when he fell down some stairs. Good story, except a pickaxe won't send pieces of canvas into bones in the middle of your foot. The Doc called it in, but the greasy punk took off. He ended up dead in the van before we could bring him in. Dead from two more bullets. That brings me to you."

"You think whoever tried to kill me with the car shot this Gonzo guy too?"

"No, I don't think that. A drunk driver hit you. You shot Gonzo with the gun you were carrying. Ballistics will prove it, once I run the gun."

"Tell me," I said.

"Tell you what?"

"I've been here a long time. Why haven't you run the gun yet?"

"Heh, you're not as dumb as I thought."

Neither are you, I thought. This cop had me dead to

rights whether he knew the whole story or not. The gun they had on me would tie me to Gonzo all right. It would also tie me to a gunfight and two bodies outside of Ave Maria, a local religious store and mob front. The fact that the gun had not yet been run through the system meant that the cop standing over me wanted something.

"Tell me," I said.

"You're not a suspect yet, just a person of interest. One word from me and the prints I took off you get attached to a murder charge. You're a person of interest *only*, for now, because you and me got similar interests."

I shifted around in the bed trying to get comfortable. When I found a spot that didn't feel like I was on a hot spike, I spoke again. "What interests are those?"

"You want to stay out of jail and I want you to stay out too."

"We do see eye to eye about that, but you can't always get what you want."

"That's a good song. Back on the island we got that record."

"What island?"

"New Zealand."

That explained the features I couldn't place.

"So did we send some fat, pale cop there, and we got you in exchange?"

"Nah, mate, I'm local. Have been for years and years."

I shifted on the bed again.

"You can't always get what you want," he sang. "But if you try some time, you get what you need. Song's true, and you're going to have to figure that out."

"So what do I have to do to get what I need?"

"Nothing too taxing. I just want a bigger fish."

"And you think I can get you one?"

"Figure you can. Found you in front of a mob den with

two abandoned cars belonging to some underworld heavy hitters. I think you know some things about some people that I don't know . . . yet."

"You think that talking to you will improve my prognosis? I'm already on a list somewhere if what you say is true. Someone will want payback, and it won't be hard to get at me when I'm chained up like King Kong."

"Good film. I even liked the remake. But that might just be me rooting for a hometown face. You ever see his *Lord of the Rings*?"

I shook my head.

"Blow your fucking socks off, ya know what I mean? That was epic, just epic. Not like you, you're not epic. You're not even on anyone's radar. No one even knows you're here outside of Miller and me."

"The nurses," I said.

"We fed them a lie about you being a cop killer."

"Explains the violence and why they let it happen," I said, nodding.

"Some in the west just don't appreciate Maori medicine. To them you're just passing through. You're not even worth their time, and they won't miss you when you're gone. There's no one to miss anyway: you're not even in the system yet, and as far as the Italians know, the drunk driver outside Domenica's hit a bum, not far off on that one, eh? But you're on my shit list, and you'll be there until you give me something better to spend my time on. If you don't come up with a name for me, I'll hunt you down with a blue army behind me, and I'll make sure the Italians aren't far behind. Your best bet is to help me out and then get the hell out of town, mate."

"You're some cop, Serpico."

"I'm local, but I still got some of the old island ways inside me." He accelerated fast to his feet and hit his chest

9

with a closed fist. The sound echoed off the tight walls. His face became wildly expressive as his tongue shot out to his chin and his fist rose in the air. It was something that could have looked ridiculous, but this imposing man had the eyes of a believer. His display of the old ways was an eye opener. This man wasn't soft, he had a fire inside that hardened him. This ritual showed me what he was underneath the suit and cop shield. I understood the cop, but I wouldn't let him know.

"That dance mean it's going to rain?"

"That is no dance. It is part of the peruperu. It brings the god of war. It's the old, old ways."

"You think what I can tell you will lead you to war?"

"I don't want you to talk to me. I said I want you to get me a fish, not draw me a map to the fucking watering hole."

"How can I get you anything from here?"

"You got a few days to figure out how you can get me what I need. After that, I just process you and take what I can get with the prints on the gun. I don't care how you do it, just try not to break any more laws getting me what I want. I'd hate to have to arrest you again. You'd hate that too, that Maori medicine is a bitch the second time around."

The big cop got up and reached inside his jacket. His hand came out with a white business card. He handed it to me and then bent to plug the heart monitor back in. The machine said its thank you in steady electronic beats.

"Call the number on the back when you get me my fish. Wait too long, and the picture we took of you while you were out will start making the rounds at roll call; your prints will go into the machine too."

I didn't watch the cop leave. I studied what he had

handed me instead. Detective Sergeant Huata Morrison's card had two numbers on it — business and cell. It was a generic cheap business card, thin and plain. The only exception was the handcuff key taped to the back.

pulled the key off the back of the card and fit it into the cuffs with my right hand. I managed to find a position where I could use my thumb and index finger to turn the key. I felt the mechanism start to slowly turn and the cuffs begin to release. I opened the cuffs slowly, one size at a time until I could slip my hands from the metal rings with little friction. I couldn't walk out right away — there were too many people around, not to mention the fact that all I had to wear was the thin, assless hospital gown I had on. If I could get clothes, I could get to the car. The Volvo I rode into town on should still be parked close to Ave Maria. Its years of wear and tear would make it virtually unnoticeable in the urban jungle. It was like a boxy European mechanical tiger hiding in the long concrete grass. No one saw it coming and no one saw it go. Under the hood, the car was all after-market improvements. It would give any souped-up sports car on the road a run for its money. The car was more than a conveyance; it was a temporary bank too. In a compartment inside the trunk, under the spare, lay a few hundred thousand in cash in a fireproof box. Paolo Donati had put me in a dangerous spot a few years back. I left the city in a hurry with enough travelling money to last me years. Paolo found me in two, and I brought the balance back across the country with me, just in case I had to buy my freedom or the bullets I would need to take it. I never planned to be in town for more than a few days, so I never set up a safe place to stash the cash. I had to be prepared to leave without more than a second's notice, and I couldn't afford to leave my money behind. My need outweighed the danger of leaving all of my eggs in one basket.

If the car was still there, the spare key would be with it. I would have money and transportation. With that, I could get everything else.

The artificial light in the room gave me no sense of what time it was. The fluorescent bulbs hummed constantly, letting anyone who opened the door see me without getting too close. It could have easily been seven in the morning or seven at night. I would have to wait for visiting hours to end and the night shift to begin before I could move. The only distinction between day and night came from the interruptions caused by shift change. I always had a sense that the night shift started when there was a long lull between suspicious nurses looking in on me. The night shift was run at its own pace. Nurses came more infrequently and did their best to let the patients sleep; they tried even harder to ignore me. It would be the best time for me to slip out.

I didn't think my guard would be with me in the room anymore. He was waiting for me to wake up so that I could be interrogated. Now that I was conscious, and my interrogation had been completed by the big cop Morrison, I figured the plan would be to leave me to heal before I was fed to the system.

14

I closed my eyes and relaxed. I was sore everywhere, but I could still move. Some of the bumps I took before the accident seemed not to hurt as much as I remembered. I checked every body part with a movement starting from the top. My scan halted when I moved my hips and felt discomfort from the catheter. The tube hurt, and I knew it would have to come out. I slid my right hand free under the sheet and felt around my dick. There was nothing permanent holding the tube in place; that meant there was something anchoring it inside my bladder. I would have to dismantle the urinary device, but that would have to wait until I was ready to check out.

My mind raced. I had let Paolo Donati control me, and it had cost me. I was in the city because he forced me, to come home, and I spent every moment of my return playing keep up. I had to juggle Paolo, his threats, his job, and his timetable in order to survive. I had managed to hand Paolo over to Julian to end the juggling, but I had still wound up behind the eight ball. A drunk driver was an 80 km/h monkey wrench. Everything I worked for, the life under the radar and off the grid, compromised because of some asshole overdoing it during happy hour. I let myself give in and feel all the rage inside. My fists clenched, and I felt my nails pierce the skin of my palms. After ten long seconds, I let everything go and started planning.

When the day shift ended, I would move. I didn't know my way around, but I had no time to reconnoitre. I had to play everything by ear. I went over everything I knew about hospitals in my head. There were both elevators and stairs on each floor. Each ward was usually broken down into patient rooms, offices, supply cupboards, and a central desk for admitting patients and keeping track of the streams of information passing from machines, to doctors, to nurses, and finally back to machines again. To get out to the elevators or stairs, I would at least have to pass the nurses at the front desk. Any movement would be trouble; the staff had been informed that I was a suspect in a murder, and that fat cop had camped out in the room with me for days. The staff would be on edge about my presence, more so now that it was common knowledge that I was conscious. Hospital security would not be far away from my door; I was probably a stop on some guard's nightly rounds. I lay in the bed and thought about my options until my eyes caught sight of something on the ceiling — a smoke detector burrowed into the faded ceiling panels above me. Smoke detectors were in every room, and they connected to a loud alarm. I imagined that hospital protocol would demand an evacuation if a fire threatened the patients. Alarms brought chaos, chaos brought confusion, and confusion brought a smile to my face.

With a plan formed in my mind, I relaxed a little more. I spent the rest of the day in and out of sleep. When I was out of dream land, I occupied myself by bopping my head to the beat of the heart monitor or holding my breath to see how fast I could make it go.

My games were interrupted by a doctor and nurse who entered together.

"What time is it?" I asked.

The doctor looked put out. "A little after five, almost dinner. Now that you're awake, you can eat tonight. Er, well," he stuttered, looking at my chains, "someone from security can aid you in your eating."

"Any chance you can get these off?"

Zero hesitation came with the answer. "No."

"Fine. What hospital am I in?"

"St. Joseph's, Mr. . . . ah, I don't have a name for you. It would seem that you were brought in without any identification. What is your name?"

"James. James Moriarty." The name wasn't mine. But it served the man who evaded Sherlock Holmes well. Someone would find humour in the name eventually. It wouldn't be funny at first, but once I got loose and disappeared someone would chuckle under their breath about it.

"Well, Mr. Moriarty, is there any chance that you know your health card number?"

"Not off the top of my head."

"Social Insurance number then?"

"Starts with a five. Second number is a four. Does that help?"

"No. Well, you look fit, I'll see about food being sent round. Need to keep your strength up for the trial."

The nurse let the doctor out of the room first. As he passed, she paused to sneak a look in my direction. I winked, and she jumped as though she had been Tasered in the ass.

The door closed, and I was left alone with the beeps. Hours passed, and food never arrived. I wasn't surprised. Labelled as a cop killer, I was sure to be on everyone's shit list. If food did show up, I wouldn't eat it. I would fake stomach troubles to avoid the real ones that would surely come later from eating a tampered dinner. The noise in the hall got quieter and quieter as visiting hours waned. Eventually, it took minutes for me to hear any sound at all. A nurse poked her head in and looked me over from the door while I pretended to sleep. She left the room without turning off the lights. It was like that every night. I was constantly on display under the never-ending fluorescent glare of the lights so that none of the nurses would have to step into the room to get a look at me pretending to sleep.

I used the catheter, gritting my teeth the whole time at the plastic handcuff that locked my dick to the bed. I had to wait a bit longer.

My wait was interrupted by a nurse tumbling into the room ass first. She hit the ground and shuffled backwards across the floor to the wall as the man who pushed her entered. Behind the man was a young woman.

"Fuck your visiting hours. We are not here to visit. We are here to make things even."

I knew the face. The Russian accent spun the Rolodex in my mind to the name that matched the mug — Igor. I had shot Igor in the shoulder a few years back when he had tried to kill me in my office. Igor and another hench-man had shown up to find out what I knew about the robbery of some Russian property, and he ended up on the wrong side of a bullet. Igor failed his boss and named names to me. I let him and his partner live to save me the trouble of disposing of their bodies. For betraying his boss, I figured he'd have to hide out for the rest of what should have been his short life.

"What? You don't remember me, mystery man?"

"I remember you, Igor. I thought you'd have been smart enough to hitch a ride out of town on the Siberian Express."

"Leave? Why would I be leaving? You killed Mikhail. That was a big favour. No one knew who he sent out to see you, so I was in the clear. And because you killed Gregor too, I was the only one who knew what had happened."

"So it was me who killed your partner?" Igor was lying — running some kind of game. I killed Mikhail, but Gregor walked out of my office with Igor.

He turned to the dirty-blond-haired woman behind him. He laughed in her direction, and she replied in kind.

"You see, baby? He is a worthless liar, a dog. He kills Gregor, and he can't even man up to it. Not even at the end."

The dirty-blond was five-ten and dressed in the finest

clothes the girls' department could offer. Everything was too tight. Underneath her open jacket I could see her breasts spilling over the bra cups. The jeans had a big "I" belt buckle above the zipper. The buckle was studded with glittering crystals and was ornamental only. The jeans cut into her flesh and made the flab on her stomach spill over the material. The belt buckle was Igor's way of branding the girl. He showed the world she was his with his very own tacky mark.

"Introduce us, Igor."

He chuckled. "This is Tatiana. Tatiana, this is a dead man."

Tatiana smiled at me, then winked at Igor.

"How'd you find me, Igor? You're a low-level fish, and I'm not even sure you know my name."

The fish comment pissed him off. "I am no fish, and your name is not important. One of my own little fish told me about some murders outside of a club we know. I came to see who was involved, because perhaps the people I work for could benefit from such information. Information pays highly, but it turns out that it is me who will be benefiting and you who will be paying. Your name is not important to me because you will be dead and forgotten in a few moments."

"See, you *are* low level fresh off the dock fish. The scared nurse on the ground has more intel than you."

Igor reached into his right jacket pocket and freed a snub-nosed revolver. The draw was fast because the front sight on the gun had been filed down. Igor had never graduated to a holster. He was still carrying guns in his pockets like a fourteen-year-old on his first stick-up. Despite the fact that he had found me, Igor was still unprofessional.

"What is his name?" he said, pointing the gun at the nurse on the floor.

"James . . . James Moriarty."

"See? A gun is like information ATM. It gets me everything I need. We are all friends now. *Da?*" He smiled a crooked smile at me. The smile was the work of shitty Russian dentistry. When he laughed, I caught a glimpse of shiny stainless steel teeth glinting from the back of his mouth.

"How'd you find me, Igor?"

"When you left, you killed important men in our organization. Positions had to be filled. Sergei Vidal recognized my useful skills, and I was promoted. I now do what Mikhail did."

I was amazed at how different mobs from different cultures managed to operate synchronously. The Italians under Paolo Donati made similar promotions when the Russians had decimated their ranks. It was the premature elevation of the new generation that led to his nephews being kidnapped and eventually his death. It looked like the Russians promoted the same breed of youngster when they faced similar losses. Mikhail had run a neighbourhood until we crossed paths. Sergei Vidal, the highest ranking Russian crime boss in the city, cut me a deal after I killed Mikhail. He promised me that we would be square if I got him back some disks I stole. I got most of the disks back, keeping only one for personal insurance. Sergei and I were in a stalemate last I checked. Igor's visit said different.

"So you came here thinking you could sell some information to Sergei? Some promotion you got — you're nothing like Mikhail; he was management, you're just an errand boy. Do you think Sergei would still let you be his bitch if he knew how badly you screwed up the first time you came after me?"

"There you go lying again." Igor aimed the pistol at my head from five feet away from the bed. If I slipped out of the loosened cuffs, I'd still be too far away to stop him

MIKE KNOWLES

from killing me. "You see, Tatiana? He lies right until the very end."

"Just pull the trigger, baby. I want to see you kill him."

"Tatiana, you ever see him with his shirt off?" I asked.

She didn't answer. She instead looked to Igor with confusion on her face. I could tell she wanted to know what I meant, but Igor was running the show, so she looked to him.

"Go wait in the car!"

"But you said I could watch. You promised, baby."

Igor slapped her with the back of his empty left hand. She grunted with the impact, but she didn't cry out.

"I knew you would chicken out. You always chicken out. You are like a little . . ."

Igor punched Tatiana in the stomach and she crumpled to the floor. She was allowed less than a second to rest before he pulled her up by her hair. "You shut up and get out! I don't explain myself to you, whore. Do as I say and get in the car. Do not let anyone see you, understand?"

Tatiana had nothing else to say; she just nodded, turned around, her head hung low, and walked towards the door. She looked over her shoulder at Igor and caught sight of the nurse on the floor.

"What are you looking at?"

The nurse started to stammer out a response, but Tatiana's shoe cut her off. The nurse back crawled into the corner of the room as she tried to avoid the kicks. Isolated, with no where else to go, she covered her head and cried. Tatiana kicked the nurse until Igor pulled her away and shoved her towards the door.

"I told you to get the fuck out of here."

Tatiana took one last look at the nurse's body — the woman was still sitting up but no longer conscious — and went out into the darkened hallway.

"You two have a real future, Igor."

"Shut up."

"Hard to call me a liar when I know about the bullet hole I put in your left shoulder."

"Shut up, you motherfucker! No more talk."

"If you kill me, Igor, my deal with Sergei is done."

He paused and squinted at me, over the barrel of the gun, confused by my words.

"Deal?"

"Sergei and I are square. You not knowing that means you aren't high enough on the totem pole to be pulling any triggers. You know that though, don't you? Makes me wonder why you're ready to shoot me in the middle of a hospital without permission from your boss."

"Revenge. You cost me everything."

"Sounds to me like I gave you everything. I let you live and I killed your boss. If you took over for Mikhail, you run a neighbourhood now. You're something of a player because of me."

"All that means nothing without closure. Everything I earned, and I earned it, means nothing without getting the closure I need. I can't do my job right, I can't earn, I can't even fuck! What you did to me ruined me, and I can't get past it. I need other people to do everything for me. Do you know how hard it is to come up with reasons why you can't work? It's exhausting. I'm always . . ." he motioned his hands up and down until he found the word, "juggling reasons and excuses. I need to get out of the cycle, but I won't be able to get my head right until I get back what you took from me."

Igor took a breath and wiped tears from his face. He dried his hand on his pants, then took a two-handed grip on the butt of the gun. He closed one eye and levelled the barrel with my forehead. The gun trembled a little at first, then more and more. He was working up his nerve, and he would get there unless I pushed him off course. Igor used the term "closure"; the word sounded strange coming from the gangster's mouth. He said the word slowly as though it were a serious matter. I focused on the term and used it to try to pull Igor off track.

"Killing me like this is not going to give you closure. What are you proving by just pulling the trigger while I'm chained down? You did none of the heavy lifting. Someone else did everything for you again, and you're just going to take the credit. No wonder you can't get it up; you can't even hold a gun straight."

"Shut up."

"You think Tatiana is downstairs checking out the real men?"

"Shut up."

"Men who can do their jobs. Men who fuck their women instead of beat them. Men who don't cry themselves to sleep at night."

"Shut up!"

"You don't like what I'm saying? Then prove you're better. Prove it, you limp dick." Under the covers my hands slid out from the cuffs. "Don't just pull some trigger and let the bullet do the work like everyone else does. Do something for yourself."

The trembling hands got worse, and the barrel shook away from its path to my forehead. Instead of a bullet exploding towards me, the squat revolver accelerated towards my face. Igor swung his arm up, as he advanced on me, preparing to pistol whip me.

"Shut up! Shut up!"

My hand met the Russian's wrist as it came down at my skull. My other hand grabbed the barrel of the gun and forced it up to the ceiling. I kept pushing the gun forward towards his wrist until it broke free of his grip. Igor, wild with rage, drove his head forward into my nose. I turned my head enough to take the blow on the side of my forehead. The head butt caused me to lose my grip on the gun, and it fell to the sheets. Igor's hands found my throat, and he bore down on me.

"Shut up! Shut up!"

His eyes were wild, and he was foaming at the corners of his mouth. I had coaxed him to move on me, and I was paying the price. The choke was strong, but I had been in worse scrapes with better men. I didn't waste time searching for the gun or working on the fingers of the hands on my windpipe. My left hand took a handful of hair, and my right formed an index finger fishhook. I gouged into Igor's mouth, hooking the soft flesh surrounding his bared teeth, and ripped away. His cheek tore, and Igor wailed. The sudden pain cut through the temporary insanity and broke the chokehold. Igor recoiled in pain, grabbing at his face as he lost his balance on the bed. He rolled to the floor while I sat up and grabbed the gun. The fat black revolver was ugly-beautiful, and it fit my hand like a glove on a cold winter day. I put my feet on the ground for the first time in days and felt the cold touch of the floor tiles. Air flowed up into the gown, and I felt my skin tighten. Igor still pawed at his cheek, trying to hold the newly separated flesh together while he screamed. His screams were dampened by his hands over his mouth, and the sounds came out as muffled grunts. Blood was streaming down Igor's wrists and dripping through his cupped hands onto the floor. I took a fistful of Igor's hair and pulled his head forward so that the blood stayed off his clothes. He yelped a little louder in pain for a second, then the butt of the revolver put him to sleep.

MIKE KNOWLES

When the adrenaline receded I became suddenly aware of the pull from under my gown. The catheter line was taut, and the pain radiated into my core. I had no idea how the plastic line was forced into me, and I learned the hard way, after one painful pull, that there was some sort of anchor inside my bladder holding the tube inside me. However the tube was locked in place, the bag couldn't come with me. I pawed Igor's pockets looking for a knife but found only car keys. I used the sharpest key to saw at the tube just above the bag. It took thirty seconds for the dull key to wear down the medical plastic. I threw the bag in a medical waste disposal box and gave removing the tube one last try. The catheter retracted with my pull, and I grunted as each centimetre of the tube came free. When the catheter was all of the way out, I saw that the anchor that once held it in place was now a flaccid balloon tinted pink with a sheen of blood and urine.

Free from the catheter, I wasted no time stripping Igor.

Within minutes, I was wearing his fashionable jeans and leather jacket. I also felt the bulge of his wad of cash in the pants and the weight of his revolver under my new belt.

Igor was unconscious in my gown. I bent at the waist and picked him up. It wasn't pretty; I kept the Russian face down, using his waist and a handful of hair to lift him, to avoid any more blood on the clothes. I flopped his slackened body on the bed and roughly turned him over. I closed the cuffs around his wrists until I felt bone stop the mechanism. Killing Igor would bring too much heat down from both the cops and the Russians. Hurting him would have to do. The beating wasn't severe enough to do him any serious harm; the further damage to his psyche was another story altogether.

I checked the nurse's pulse and found her to still be soundly out. I left her where she was and creaked the door open. The halls were dark and empty save the sound of two women talking somewhere down the corridor. I tilted my head out, but I couldn't see the owners of the two voices. I looked back at the nurse on the floor behind me and watched her stillness. It wouldn't last forever. If she made enough noise coming to, or anyone peeked in and saw her — the hospital would be in lockdown fast.

"Fuck," I said under my breath. I pulled the gun from under the coat and gripped the barrel. I walked over to the nurse and looked at her closely. She was beaten up, but she would live. I dragged her body behind the other side of the bed so that no one would prematurely rouse her from her concussed dreams either.

I turned off the lights in the room, eased the door open again, and saw that the hall was still clear. I walked down the corridor, away from the voices, and took the first stairwell I saw. I took the stairs down to the main floor and found another set of stairs leading to the parking garage.

All at once the steps were concrete and coated in chewed gum and grime. The light fixtures followed suit and became suddenly more sparse and cheap, offering light only on each landing. I took the first exit into the parking garage. The lot reeked of urine and mildew, and I breathed deep, enjoying the scent of the city. Even in someone else's clothes and wanted by both sides of the law, I couldn't shake the nostalgic smell of the city. Fuck freshly baked bread, it had nothing on the city air.

I walked through the rows of cars, down the ramps, to the exit. There were no security guards, only an electric arm to guard against anyone trying to sneak out without paying for parking. I didn't even break pace, just ducked under the arm and strode to the crosswalk. St. Joseph's was just outside downtown and close to everything. It was a short walk down St. Joseph's Drive to James Street. The road was busy with young people making their way into the downtown core for fun on Hess Street or in the dozens of pubs located on every other block.

The streetlights were on, and I was sure that the stars were out above the layer of constant pollution in the sky. I put a kilometre of distance between the hospital and myself before stopping on the curb. I waited two minutes for a cab to come down the mountain access, past the hospital, on its way to drunken downtown fares. I stepped out in front of the cab and got in the back while the cabby got over his shock.

"You can't jump in front of cars like that! You'll get hit!"

"Take me to the north end of Wentworth."

"Seriously, what the fuck were you thinking?"

"Drive to Wentworth, or I step out in front of another cab."

"Fine, asshole. Whatever."

As we drove, the cab driver ran through the list of

pedestrian-initiated accidents he had seen. I didn't participate in the conversation. Once I saw that his dashboard clock read 11:38, I just kept my eyes peeled for an open store and for Ave Maria. As we clocked down Wentworth, I saw empty storefront after storefront. I almost missed Ave Maria; its old dark brick camouflage blended into the city too well. I let two streets go by before telling the cabby to turn off the road onto a quiet side street. We made two right turns before making our way behind Ave Maria. I watched the alleys and side streets as the cab got closer to the Volvo. One hundred metres away from the car, backed into an alley, I saw it. There was a dark sedan parked in the shadows. A small orange glow pierced through the dark and gave away someone sitting inside. I knew someone would be watching the alley. Before my hospital stay, I had killed two people there and maimed another. Someone would have noticed my work, and they would have eventually picked up on the Volvo collecting dust just down the street. I was sure it had been searched, but that didn't bother me; the money was well hidden. No one doing a fast street search would find it unless they knew exactly where to look. There was a chance the car would be conveniently "stolen," but if that happened, no one would be able to get a look at the owner. Whoever was watching the car was looking for some face time — probably the bloody kind. The watcher in the car was a low-level grunt, either cop or robber. Whoever they were, they would need to be dealt with if I was going to get back what was mine. And I was going to get what was mine.

"I need to get to a Shoppers Drug Mart. One of those huge twenty-four-hour stores. You know where one is?"

"As long as you promise not to get hit by a car in the parking lot."

"I promise, mom."

"Mom! Listen. I'm just trying to do my civic duty. I see too much stupid crap night after night to stay quiet. But you, you don't care. So do what you want. Lay in the street if you feel like it. I don't care anymore."

"The street would be quieter."

"All right, pal. I get it. You don't want an earful from me on your dollar. Just make sure you don't end up getting a bumperful, okay?"

"You wouldn't have hit me," I said.

"What makes you so sure?"

"I've already gotten my surprises for the day. Three in a row, God ain't that funny."

The cab driver made a confused grunt, then shut up and drove in silence. The Shoppers was on Main. It was one of the old-school stores that used to be a Big V before it was bought out. I paid the cab driver to wait out front while I went inside. The $400 I took off Igor would pay for everything I would need.

The store was a ghost town. The cashier, a fat woman with short blond hair and several moles, said, "Hello," without looking up from her magazine, and I grunted a matching response in the direction of the greeting. I walked through the aisles, skimming through all of the logically assorted items until I found what I was looking for in the small home improvement section. I picked up a roll of duct tape and an exacto-knife. A gas can also caught my eye, and I put it under my arm. A few aisles away, I found a thin baby blanket, a duffel bag, and a black baseball cap.

I paid in cash for everything I picked up and added a Nestea from the refrigerator beside the register, a package of mixed nuts, and a Three Musketeers to my purchase.

Back in the cab, I put on the hat and loaded the duffel bag while we drove back to James Street. When we pulled to a stop across the street from where I was first picked up, I paid the cab driver.

"Now you watch out for pedestrians."

"Me? Me? It is you who should be watching out. You walked in front of me right over there. Remember? I almost . . ."

I shut the door and walked back to the hospital. Instead of going to the parking garage I came out of, I walked to the front of the hospital. The lot was half full of cars despite the late hour. The cars were empty, and I saw no sign of anyone leaving the building as I approached. The half-empty lot meant that no one had found Igor or the nurse yet. There was an attendant in a booth collecting tickets, but no other security backed the lone worker up. The lot had no outdoor cameras mounted to protect the cars either. The hospital must have thought that the presence of a human being would cancel out the temptation of a new BMW alone out in the open. Whoever was in the booth was old hat at the job. I could see him leaning back in a chair with a newspaper spread in front of his face. The attendant never noticed me walking across the lot into the decorative foliage on the other side of the concrete. I took a spot between two large evergreen trees and ate the mixed nuts and candy bar. I didn't take a sip of the iced tea; I left the glass bottle of Nestea at my feet.

I waited and ate until sirens began approaching from all directions. The parking lot attendant saw the rapid approach and raised the wooden bar for the cops. Five squad cars raced into the lot and took the handicap spaces. I picked around for cashews while the five cars shed their uniformed occupants. Eight cops in all ran into the hospital. The door was held open for them by an out-of-shape security guard who knew that the police presence meant it was time for him to get off his ass. He held the door and looked official until the men passed, then he just looked put out. I had finished the cashews and moved on to Brazil nuts when another car showed up. The car was not a squad car, it was a police sedan. It had no markings to establish its credentials, only the generic Ford features that let everyone know what kind of car it really was. As the car passed me, I saw the safety barrier for transporting suspects. I also noticed that Detective Sergeant Huata Morrison was driving. He paused in front of the entrance and put the car in park, but a security guard opened the door, pointed at the no stopping signs, and waved him away. Morrison put the Ford into gear and drove into the lot to find a spot.

I left my spot among the trees and walked onto the lot. From his booth the attendant couldn't see me moving out of my spot in the shadows. His back was to me, and his eyes were on something in his hands. He was probably on a cell phone — texting someone about the action.

Morrison found a spot in the middle of the lot and pulled in headfirst so that the car faced the hospital entrance. I was ten metres away when he opened the door. I sped up my pace and closed the gap as he put one foot on the pavement. Morrison put down his other foot and got out of the car dragging his suit jacket along with him. His back was to me as he put the jacket on. His broad shoulders made it difficult, and he had to raise one arm high in the air to slide the jacket over his shoulders. His stance was wide, and just as his suit jacket slid on, my foot connected with his groin. Morrison had no time to scream because my arm was around his windpipe before he hit the ground. My right hand found my biceps, and my left hand went behind the big man's head. The rear naked choke was textbook; the kick to the balls left the cop defenceless, and it let me get in tight. His powerful frame surged against the choke for a few seconds, but the hold won quickly. Some people can fight a sloppy choke for as long as they can hold their breath, but a good choke doesn't attack the airway. The flesh and bone vise around Morrison's neck cut off circulation, not oxygen, and no one can hold out against a loss of blood to the brain for more than a few seconds. I kept the choke on for another fifteen seconds before letting it go in favour of a grip under the sagged shoulders of the big cop. I backed into the car first and pulled Morrison into the driver's seat.

It took under two minutes to tape Morrison into the car. He was straight up in the seat, duct taped to the headrest. The tape covered his forehead and eyebrows; another section of tape secured his throat to the seat as well. Both of the cop's hands were attached to the steering wheel at ten and two. I turned out all of Morrison's pockets and put his phone, wallet, and gun on the dashboard in front of me; then I drank the Nestea and checked the lot. No one else had shown up, and no one had left the hospital. The lot was quiet; the only interruption came from the cell phone. Morrison's phone was on vibrate, and it marched across the dashboard like an angry bee buzzing in an out-of-control fit. The phone call was expected; I figured the first response cops were waiting for Morrison to show up and take control of the situation. He was late to the party, and someone wanted to know why. I took one last swig of iced tea and dumped the rest into Morrison's lap. He came to slowly at first, then all at once. His eyes went wild, and he strained against the tape. I let him pull and yell for a minute, then I let him feel his gun against his neck.

"You! What the fuck are you doing? I'll get you for this. I'm gonna lock you up and fucking eat the key. Hey, what are you doing?"

I put two pieces of tape over his mouth and nose and

MIKE KNOWLES

watched him struggle. He pulled so hard at his bonds that the steering wheel started to creak.

I pulled the tape off with one quick motion and heard a huge gasp of air.

"That Maori medicine is no fun, eh, Detective Sergeant?"

"I'm a cop," was all he could get out.

"And here I thought you were a fisherman looking for the big catch. Or was that all bullshit? You just let me think I was supposed to be working for you while you tipped off your boss. Way I figure it, you were the only one who knew who I was. You don't even really know that, but you got ideas about me that aren't far off. So you tip off the Russians, and you earn yourself a bonus giving me up."

"I don't know what you're talking about."

"The only thing I can't figure is why you left me a hand-cuff key. Have the Russians got something on you? You're into them for some big numbers, and you thought I might kill whoever is holding your bill and end your troubles?"

"No idea, mate. I have no idea what you are going on about. What Russians? I got called back here because they found you gone and a nurse dead in your room."

"Dead? How?"

"Someone cut her throat."

"Hard for me to do in a gown."

"Heh, you seem to be managing," he said.

"If you didn't tip the Russians, who did?"

"I don't know."

"Who knew I wasn't a cop killer like you said?"

"No one outside of me and Miller."

"That fat cop?"

"Yeah, but he's straight."

"Well, two people knew I was there, and you said it wasn't you who gave me up. It's got to be him; probably made the call on one of his smoke breaks."

Morrison said nothing. If he was telling the truth, and my gut told me he was, then it was Miller who was crooked. The fat cop made more sense; no one would give me a way out of the cuffs if I was worth more dead than alive. Miller must be the one on the take. Once he was off guarding my unconscious body, he told the Russians about me, hoping I was someone recognizable, to make a little extra. He figured since they found me outside Domenica's, and his boss was having me guarded, I must be worth something. So Miller reached out to Igor. He had to work directly for Igor in one form or another because anyone else would have sent the information up the chain to Sergei Vidal. Had Sergei found out, I would have been safe. The head of the Russian mob and I still had an understanding. I had enough evidence on him to send him away for life. I figured our deal was still in place because if Sergei wanted to end it he would never have sent Igor to punch my ticket. Sergei would have dispatched someone closer to the top with orders to kill me. I'd gone up against Sergei's best before — they would have done better than Igor.

Morrison was quiet and motionless in the seat beside me.

"You still want your fish?"

"You're the fish now. You have to pay for that nurse."

"Use your head, Morrison. I didn't kill anyone. I got a visit from a Russian, someone who knew me and wanted to settle up old debts. He tried to kill me, but I talked him out of it — with my hands. When I left, he was on the bed, and the nurse was very much alive. If you check the bed, there will be blood from the Russian to back up my story."

"Bullshit."

"You know it sounds right. Why else would I be here now?"

MIKE KNOWLES

"So what do you want?"

"Same deal. I get your fish, you forget about me."

"Which fish?"

"That's up to me, but I can tell you they'll be cold water fish from up near the Black Sea."

Morrison tried to nod his head in agreement, but he stopped when he realized he couldn't move. "It will have to be one big fish to square everything."

"Let me worry about that. I just need some information from you."

"What?"

"Where do the Russians go these days? The only place I knew was the Kremlin, but it's probably gone."

"Yeah, someone shot that place up a few years back; killed a bigwig." A thought came to Morrison; I watched it form in a series of facial twitches. "That was you. That's why the Russians showed up tonight. Word on the street was that was some kind of internal cleaning thing."

I ignored him. He had a real cop's mind. He listened, and he remembered. I had to make sure I gave away nothing because even taped to the seat this cop was dangerous. I repeated myself, "Where do the Russians meet these days? Where do all the big names end up at the end of a long, hard day of crime?"

Morrison thought about it. "There are three places," he said. "There's a hall on Sanford, a restaurant on St. Claire, and a bar on Sherman where it meets Barton."

"All the big names congregate in these places?"

"Congregate? Look at you. Mate, you are one educated thug. I don't think I've heard that word since Sunday school. No, wait — that was congregation. Mean the same thing, ya reckon?"

The cop was still filing away everything I said, stringing clues together into a noose. I grinned in approval towards the window so he wouldn't see. The silence hung in the air until he answered my question.

"If we lose any of the major players, or we need to pick up a tail, it's where we start looking."

"Keep your phone on, I've got your number," I said as I got out of the car.

"Hey! Hey, let me loose before you rack off. Hey!"

I walked back to the evergreens, away from the screams of Detective Sergeant Huata Morrison. I walked straight through the sparsely planted trees and out the other side. I jogged down James Street, away from the hospital, and into the first bar I saw. The dingy clock on the wall read 12:58. I ordered a Diet Coke and called a cab.

By the time the ice in my Diet Coke had melted, the cab had shown up, and I was off. I had the cabbie take me to a gas station that sold cell phones. The drive took us all the way into Westdale, a ritzy suburb of Hamilton that had old money and the university.

I filled the gas can I'd bought earlier and went inside to buy a lighter and a prepaid cell phone. The Asian man and woman behind the counter gladly accepted my money and slowly made change while their black cat walked across my path over the top of the gum display. By the time the change was in my palm, the cat was at my feet — rubbing its back against my leg. I pushed the cat away with Igor's shoe. The cat rolled to its feet and rose — tensed. Its back was high, and each hair bristled in anticipation of a fight. Teeth were showing, and a guttural hissing climbed up out of the cat's mouth.

The lady behind the counter looked upset. "You no like cat?"

"No, I don't like the cat."

"Why not? You think cat got bad luck?"

MIKE KNOWLES

"I don't know if a cat crossing my path is bad luck, but fuck him if he wants to try and rub it against my leg."

"Hunh?"

"He wants to ruin my day, he's gotta work for it like everyone else."

No one wished me a good night when I left.

CHAPTER FOUR

Back in the cab, I set up the phone and called the operator to test the signal. The electronic voice of the operator let me know everything worked. I powered down the phone and watched Westdale slip away. The rich houses and profitable small businesses slowly turned to rotted buildings and vacant storefronts. I had dreams that went like that. Everything good flying away like shrapnel while I watched from inside a cage. My parents went first, then my uncle. The only thing left was me. Dreams like that pushed me to make sure that there was nothing left to lose.

I succeeded for a time; nothing touched me. But over time, my guard wore down, and Steve and Sandra, a local bartender and his wife, became my friends. A few years back, one of Paolo's men, Tommy Talarese, tried to destroy their lives, and as a result he set in motion a chain of events that rocked the underbelly of the city. Tommy Talarese wanted to show his kid how to collect protection like a man after Steve had thrown the kid out into the street. They kidnapped Steve's wife, unleashing the bar owner like a wiry hurricane on the neighbourhood. Steve and I worked our way up the chain of local muscle to Tommy's front door. Many died getting Sandra back. I put everything on the line for them that night and made enemies with the Italians.

Steve and Sandra were two people, like my parents, who wouldn't give in. Two people who lived life on their own terms, who refused to let anyone, even mobsters, control their lives. I envied their freedom, their connection, and I made sure they kept it. By protecting their connection, it became my own. They were my weakness, and Paolo Donati exploited it. The old Italian boss used them to get me under his thumb again. I had gotten out and started a life away from what I had been — until a man came calling with a message. Paolo could touch me no matter how far I ran, and he could touch Steve and Sandra too. I was forced to come back to work a job for Paolo. Someone had kidnapped his nephews, and he feared it was someone on the inside. Paolo needed me, an outsider, to look into his own men. I found out who killed his nephews and arranged a meeting with Paolo. With Paolo gone, I wouldn't make the same mistake. I would leave Steve and Sandra out of this — I had learned that being my friend had worse odds than terminal cancer.

After fifteen minutes of driving, the cab neared Ave Maria and my car. We passed the front of the store, and I told the cab driver to pull over. It was two in the morning, and the street was empty. I got out with my things and walked to the driver side window to pay.

"Thirty even, pal."

I showed him the gun I took off Igor. "I got a .38. Can you make change?"

"Holy shit! Don't kill me."

Igor's ugly revolver coaxed the cab driver out of the car.

He was a squat man, five-five at the most. He wore old pleated pants and an old, out-of-style checked shirt. The pants were held up by suspenders, but they weren't the ugliest part of the outfit. On top of his head, the cab driver wore a Blue Jays cap. The front was white foam, and the back was a blue mesh. The foam-fronted hat was barely pulled down, making it look like it was ready to float away. I guessed he wore it to make him look taller — all it did was make his head look misshapen.

"Open the gas cover."

The driver leaned back in the open door and pulled at a lever. There was a metallic click behind me as the small plate unlocked and popped open. The driver stood up slowly and put his hands in the air voluntarily.

"This is like the third fuckin' time this year. Holy shit, I'm tired of people robbing me. Fuckin' knives and the '*gimme the money*.'" He mimed an impression of a stick-up and then put his hands back up. "I'm fucking tired of this shit."

"Shut up and sit on the curb."

"Do this, do that. Yes, sir, I'll do whatever you want 'cause you're the big man with the gun."

"Sit down before I put a bullet in your ass."

He sat, and I pulled the baby blanket out of the duffel bag. I soaked it with gas from the gas can until the fabric was sopping wet. I put the can down and ripped the aerial off the roof. I used the metal rod to jam the cheap wet fabric down into the gas tank. I pushed a wad in, cleared out the antenna, and then pushed another mass of blanket in again. I repeated the process until two-thirds of the blanket was gone. I left the antenna in the tank with the blanket and got behind the wheel.

"Sure, just take the car. It's not like it's my life or anything. It's just a hobby. I work double shifts until five in the morning to cut the stress."

I pulled away from the curb watching the rear-view. The cab driver got off the curb and fished through his pockets looking for a phone. I grinned because I saw the phone on the seat beside me. He was having no luck tonight either; it felt good to meet another member of the bad luck club. I drove the car down the first right and hooked onto the road that ran behind Ave Maria. I took the lighter from my pocket and held it in my fist. I forced myself to calm down and drive slowly down the road. In the alley ahead was the same dark car I passed before. This time there was no giveaway that there were any occupants inside. I drove past the alley to the Volvo and dropped the duffel bag out the window. As the bag hit the pavement, I hit the brakes, shoved the gear shifter in reverse, and forced the pedal into the floor. The car screeched back to the mouth of the alley hiding the dark car. I got out of the passenger side of the cab and flicked the lighter alive. The feeble flame shuddered as I walked before maturing into a blaze when it touched the blanket. I ran to the Volvo as I heard a car door open.

I made it to the duffel bag when the explosion sent me sailing to the pavement. I regained my footing and hustled to the car. My hand went under the wheel well and pulled free the spare key. I opened the door and threw the duffel bag across the seat hard enough to bounce it off the opposite door. The engine turned over without any coaxing, and the car roared to life. The Volvo was a different breed of animal when compared to other cars on the road. The engine was a transplant; something customized to sprint. The V8 400 horsepower engine sped me away from downtown and the mess I made, leaving only rubber behind on the pavement.

I had no idea who was watching the car. If it was the cops, the plates and the car description were whizzing past me in the air to every squad car in Hamilton. I had to get somewhere safe; somewhere I could be local while at the same time out of sight like a rabbit in a magician's hat. I hooked the car onto King Street and ran two lights. I rolled past Dundurn and floored the Volvo onto the highway putting distance between myself and the city at 140 km/h. In under a minute, I took the exit to the suburb of Ancaster and used the empty streets to drive back towards the edge of the city. I stopped on a side street before turning onto Highway Two and checked the car for bugs. I didn't want someone tracking me with a laptop to pick me up as soon as I stopped driving. When I was satisfied the car was clean, I got on the road again. I rolled down Highway Two eyeing the view off the side of the escarpment. The city of Hamilton looked full of promise from above. You couldn't see anyone hitting his wife, shooting up smack, or trying to kill a person in a hospital bed. The city from this height was a mirage.

At the bottom of the hill, I turned into the parking lot of a fleabag motel. The Escarpment was in an odd pocket of the city. There were expensive high-rises a stone's throw away in one direction and cheap apartments rented to immigrants in the other. The motel was in the middle, and its clientele leaned towards the low renters. The Escarpment Motel offered hourly rates and parking in the rear — everything I needed to stay under the radar.

I parked the car and walked into the office. A young kid sat behind the counter watching an old horror movie.

"What'cha need?"

"Room," I said.

"How long?"

"Week."

The amount of time made the kid's eyebrows raise, but his pupils never left the screen.

"Week'll cost ya two hundred bucks," the kid said as he slammed his palm around the desk beside him. His eyes were glued to the movie, and he wasn't going to miss anything. His hand stopped on a rectangular piece of paper, and his fingers traced its perimeter before picking it up. "Fill this out."

I paid with ten bills and scratched a name on the registration card. He absentmindedly handed me a key with a twelve etched on the back.

"Can I borrow a screwdriver? My luggage locked up on me, and I need to get into it so I can change."

The kid sighed and got out of his chair. He backed away from the desk and bent at the knees in a way that allowed him to keep his eyes on the television. After a minute, he found the toolbox. It took one more minute for his unguided hands to zero in on the screwdriver.

"Here," he said, throwing the screwdriver in my direction. It was a good throw considering he wasn't looking. "It's a multi-tool, so it's got everything."

"Thanks."

"Just bring it back when you're done, or I'll add it to your bill."

"Any more on the bill and you'll have to add a star to the motel."

The jab went over the kid's head, but he didn't seem bothered. He sat down and resumed his movie-watching trance.

I went out to the Volvo and drove it several doors down from the room. If anyone came looking for the car, I didn't want them using it as an arrow pointing directly to me. I used the cheap multi-tool screwdriver to take the plates off the Volvo. I took the two plates with me to the next parking lot. The apartment building next door was upscale enough to have tenants with cars, but still too shitty to provide a safe underground parking garage. I walked through the lot until I found an old car with two flat tires. No one had moved the car in months. I used the multi-tool to replace the car's plates with the Volvo's. I took the boosted plates back to the motel and completed the switch unnoticed before walking the screwdriver back.

"Thanks."

"Man, when you go back to your room, turn on channel 149. Romero is such a genius. Just look at those zombies go."

On the TV screen, two lumbering monsters chased a woman around a cage. Bloodthirsty spectators screamed bets and waved money in their fists. It was some sort of post-apocalyptic gladiator game. The girl on screen did anything but kick the shit out of her slowly approaching attackers. The game in the cage was almost at an end, when out of nowhere, except to anyone watching, a handsome man shot his way on screen and killed the two zombies. He took the girl out of the cage and backed off the angry spectators with a hard stare.

I left before I got roped into a review of the talents of George A. Romero. The carnage on the screen reminded me of something else, not a movie; I thought about the nurse who had been murdered on the floor of the hospital room. Someone had put her down after she was already out. Igor was the obvious doer, but he was chained down. That left the girlfriend. Igor sent her away, but it was probable that she was the one who came back and got Igor loose. Once he was free, either one could have dealt with the nurse. I've known enough blood-thirsty women in my life to know Tatiana was as much a suspect as her man. I let myself into the motel room and sat on the bed. Igor was damaged because I had beaten him before, and the embarrassment destroyed his ego. I had broken something in him that was always destined to give way. He blamed me for his weakness, but he was already weak when he first came at me years ago in my office. I showed him what he really was when I put him under the gun. He saw his reflection for the first time in the shine of a bullet, and what he saw didn't measure up. Plenty of people figured out they weren't cut out for the life on the same day they learned that they were just man enough to fill a grave.

In the hospital room, he lied about me killing his partner to Tatiana. The lie was as good as a confession — he was the one who had killed his partner. Igor must have done it because his partner was one of the few witnesses alive who knew he failed to do his job. He killed his partner and in that instant put on a disguise. He thought everyone bought whatever manufactured confidence he wore like too much cheap cologne. He was living a lie, and I was the only one left who knew what the lie truly was. He came to kill me so that he could fully become his false self. It was more than revenge for Igor; killing me was survival.

Whatever fragile mental case Igor was didn't matter. He found me. He was connected and just powerful enough to be a problem. Worse still was the cop. The dead nurse would put enough pressure on him to renege on our deal. I had to steel his nerve if I wanted to stay out of jail.

I stripped off Igor's clothes and lay above the covers, lights off, with Igor's gun in my hands. I slept easily because I knew what I was. I didn't lie, to myself like Igor did. I knew my nature, and I wasn't ashamed. I also knew what had to be done when the sun rose.

The next morning, my body woke itself up. I turned my head and saw the clock read 12:23. The dim room was smelly. The smell had always been there, but I was too charged up on adrenaline the night before to notice. I was also aware of my body. Morrison had told me I'd been hit by a drunk driver. Laying in a hospital bed, it didn't feel so bad, but after a night of moving I felt different. My ribs and forearms were sore, but my hip was agony. I was sure that the car had hit me there. I stood and stumbled to the washroom. I grunted and felt my dick pay me back for my medical malpractice with the catheter. It took a few seconds for the blood flowing out of me to fade into pink urine. I looked away from the mess in the bowl to the tiny square mirror hanging over the toilet. A week's worth of growth had been added to the beard I had before the accident. My hair had been clipped so short two weeks ago that the small bit of growth was unnoticeable.

I stumbled back to the bedroom, the only room, and pushed the bed up onto its side. I used the tiny bit of space on the floor to stretch. I spent an hour on the floor, stopping only when I could stand up straight without wincing, then I went back to the bathroom and washed in the cramped shower stall.

There were no towels, so I dried using the bed sheet and then put Igor's clothes back on. I walked out with the empty duffel bag and opened the trunk. Under the carpet, below the spare, was the compartment full of cash. I had not bothered to move it away from the car before because I was always just a surprise away from bolting. The money had to stay close. Now, with the car no longer anonymous, it wasn't safe to leave the money inside. I loaded the bag with the cash and walked out to a bus stop. I waited fifteen minutes inside the graffiti-tinted bus shelter for the right bus to pull to a stop. I got on and noticed that my clothes were wrinkled and stained enough to match every other jobless passenger who was riding the bus with me at 2:30 in the afternoon on a weekday.

I rode the bus up the escarpment and into the suburb of Ancaster until I saw a gym roll past the window. I got off at the next stop and walked back to the gym. The hours posted on the outside window began early and ended late. The gym was open every day at 5:30 a.m. and closed every night at midnight. Through the glass, I could see that the equipment was old, and there were few patrons inside. The time of day didn't matter; good gyms were always busy. This particular establishment was old, and they seemed to have problems keeping up with the new chains that offered a constantly changing line-up of fad activities like hip-hop Pilates. I took one last look inside before I walked back to the bus stop to wait for another ride.

At 3:30, another bus picked me up and took me to a busy commercial development on the edge of Ancaster. The strip, just off Golf Links Road, contained a store to cater to almost every human need. Within two hours, I had picked up clothes, food, toiletries, a towel, a folding knife, and a combination padlock.

I took the bus back to the gym. Phoenix Fitness was still open and still not very busy. This time I left the windows alone and walked straight inside. A kid in his twenties manned the counter, talking on the phone and drinking a health juice drink from a straw. I looked at him, and he glanced at me before waving me through and turning his back to continue his conversation.

"I got to work tonight too, yo. No, not here, at West 49. I couldn't get out of it. We'll go out after, man. I'm gonna get fuckin' tanked. I don't give a shit if I have to work tomorrow — I'll just power through. I've been hung over here before. Hell, I'm a bit hung over now. Yeah, yeah, right."

I stared at the kid's back and watched him talk. He was fit, with the kind of bulk that came from heavy daily workouts. His hair was short and styled stiff with gel, and his head bobbed with each agreement he made out loud into the phone. There was a pause in the conversation as the kid took another sip from his drink. He put the cup down beside him and laughed at a joke I couldn't hear. I was tired, not from lack of sleep or injury, just tired of assholes throwing their weight around. The jock behind the counter was just another jerk-off who thought he could push me around. I was tired of being pushed by cops and crooks and now by over-developed minimum wagers. I picked up the cup, feeling the weight of the remaining fluid inside. I stood with the drink in my hand for thirty seconds until the desire for liquid arose in the kid again. His hand began groping around the counter for the container while he spoke into the receiver. I set the drink down on the edge of the counter so that part of the cup was off the side. The phone conversation became shorter and shorter as the kid focused more and more on the missing container. After three failed gropes towards the spot the drink used to be, he turned around to see it in front of me. He stared at the drink, confused at its location, then at me to see if it was a joke. I didn't smile.

"I'll call you back," he said to whoever was on the other end of the connection.

He reached for his drink, and I shook his hand. The kid was startled by the gesture, but he recovered and pumped my hand hard with a testosterone-filled challenge. I let him squeeze with little resistance. I could have turned the handshake into something mangling, but I didn't want this kid to remember much about me.

The kid, happy with his winning grip on my loose hand, let go and gave me his best tough guy greeting. It was full of artificial street and imaginary persecution. "Wha'choo need?"

"I need a month pass. What will that cost me?"

"Cost you fifty bucks."

I peeled off a fifty and put it on the counter. He reached for the money, but my hand never moved — it stayed on top of the bill.

"This fifty get me a locker?"

"Yeah, but no spa or tanning. That stuff is extra."

I chuckled at the idea of using a spa or tanning bed. "I'll get by," I said.

The kid reached for his drink, and I met his hand with the money. He couldn't hide his disappointment as he took the money instead of his drink. I put the duffel bag on the counter in front of the drink and asked if I had to fill out a form.

"It'll be faster if I do it." Thirst had made the kid efficient. "What's your name?"

"James Moriarty," I said, expecting the question.

"Spell it."

I did. I pulled an address and phone number out of the air and listened to the kid pound the keyboard in front of him. The card printed, and the kid laminated it, stealing glances at me and the bag guarding his drink the whole time. When the card was finished, I took my bag off the counter and walked to the change room. I heard him reach for the cup and then swear as it fell to the floor. There was a splat and then more swearing as I pushed open the locker room door.

I found my locker and set my bags down on the small ledge below that was supposed to act as a bench. There was only one other person in the change room — an old man, totally nude. He slowly took a shaving kit and towel out of a locker and walked by me to the showers. He never glanced at me or attempted to hide his nakedness. He was too old to be ashamed and too tired to try to suck anything in. I waited for the shower door to close before dumping out one of the shopping bags onto the ledge. I transferred the cash from the duffel to the empty shopping bag. I set the stuffed plastic bag inside my locker and sealed the door with the brand new lock I picked up earlier. As soon as the lock clicked shut, I spun the dial through the first two numbers of the three-number code so that I could open the lock fast when I came back. I refilled the duffel bag with the things I sprawled across the ledge and walked out to the workout floor. I strolled through the gym to the back exit that was propped open to pull in cool air from outside. I left through the back door, my money safe inside a makeshift safe deposit box. The kid at the front counter would be too busy to notice that I never walked out the front door. He would just assume it happened while he was cleaning the mess from his drink. I learned that trick a decade ago as a way to swipe things from department stores. The classics never went out of style.

The bus ride back to the motel was uneventful. No one looked at me twice. I got off at the stop near the motel and walked slowly past the office. The door was open, but the guy from before wasn't there anymore. Instead, a short red-headed woman was behind the desk, television off, head down, working. I watched her stamp two pieces of paper before filing them and starting again. It was a good sign. Had anyone been around asking about me and pressing her for information, she'd have been on the lookout. Her busyness signalled everything was still kosher. The car was where I'd left it, as were the curtains. No one had done any obvious searching. I walked past the door and stopped in between my room and the next. I put my back against the wall and my hand inside my coat on top of Igor's revolver. My left hand found the key fob in my pocket and double clicked. The Volvo obediently beeped twice, calling out to the device in my hand. I watched the window, but the curtains stayed closed. I pivoted and watched the curtains in the neighbouring room, but the curtains there mimicked my own. Anyone who could have found my room would have known about the car. They would have moved on me when they heard the car out of fear of losing the advantage of surprise. Satisfied, I drew the gun, opened the door, and slipped into the darkness of the room. It took only twenty-five seconds for me to make sure the two rooms were clear.

I checked the time and got into the bathroom. I used the small mirror and sink to shave my beard to alter the appearance Igor and Morrison had seen. I put on the new clothes I had bought — dark khakis and a black T-shirt. The cooling October air would let me get away with a sweatshirt, but I went instead for a black lightweight waterproof jacket with several deep pockets. The jacket blended with the pants and concealed Igor's revolver. The Glock police pistol that I'd taken off Morrison tucked into the back of my pants, and the folding knife went into my pants pocket.

Dressed and shaved, I went out to the Volvo, got behind the wheel, and dialled Morrison. He answered after one ring. "Morrison."

"You must be out of the car."

"You son of a bitch. I'm a cop, and you pull that shit. You're done. You forgot what I got on you? When I'm done, everyone will have seen your face. It's gonna be front page, mate. You're gonna have nowhere to hide."

"You run the prints?"

"Not yet, but I'm going to. It's at the top of my to-do list right after arresting you."

"I thought you wanted a fish."

"Fuck you and your fish. You're big enough now that you killed that nurse."

"That was on you. You leaked info, and it got her killed."

"No, mate, that's not how anyone will see it. It's all about spin, and I'm gonna spin you into the ground."

"I'm sorry you feel that way."

"I bet you are."

"I'm sorry because I already got what you wanted."

"What?"

"I got your fish, and it's better than a nurse killer."

"Who is it?"

"Doesn't matter now. We're through."

"Now don't be hasty, mate. Maybe we can work something out, provided you give me something big."

"What? You'll just let me slide — I don't buy it."

"Where you're sitting right now, you've got no choice. You can be on the news tonight for sure, or maybe not at all. You serve me up something nice that I can use, and I'll be good to you. You try and dance with me again, and no amount of medicine will bring you back."

"Ten-thirty, be ready. I'll tell you where to meet me." I hung up the phone before Morrison could protest. He already had enough on me to make me an inmate for life, and showing him up in his own car hurt his pride. But angry as the cop was, he was greedy. When he found me, he knew I was into something he couldn't put his finger on. His gut told him enough about me to push him into springing me from the hospital. He was willing to go outside the law to get someone better than me. That kind of ambition was stronger than heroin; it would call to him louder than his bruised ego. It would also make him dangerous. He had no loyalty to me; I could only count on the knowledge that Morrison was only out to build himself up by taking someone else down. I had to push him off centre to get things where I needed them to be. I pulled the car out of the lot and headed to Sherman Avenue.

Morrison had said that the bar on Sherman was a

popular mob hangout. I chose the bar because it would attract the kind of people I was looking for more than the restaurant or hall he told me about ever would. I eased the Volvo through traffic until I found Barton and Sherman and the Hammer and Sickle. The bar was a single building set back from the street with a stairwell leading down to a front entrance. At street level, there were window seats behind tinted glass. There were no neon pub signs, which were so common to the bars of Hamilton, and no patio. The bar was not looking for the patronage of the locals; it catered to a specific audience who wanted nothing to do with the trendy bar scene.

I checked the mirror. No one was behind me. I slowed the car to a stop in the middle of the street and looked through the tinted bar windows. The window seats were empty, and a blond woman was wiping a table down. It was only 7:30 — still too early for the bar to be busy. There would probably be after-work drinkers inside stationed at regular seats getting a buzz to fight the tension headache brought on by sitting behind a desk all day. The people I was looking for would not be stopping by for a drink after work. By my watch, the people I wanted wouldn't start work for another few hours.

Headlights caught my eye in the rear-view, and I accelerated away from the restaurant. I turned at the corner and stopped to check out the rear lot. Of the four private parking spaces out back, three were filled with black Mercedes. The back also had a Dumpster and a rear exit door. I drove into the vacant spot and got out. The Dumpster smell hit me as soon as I touched the pavement, a sign the bar was active and not just a front. I checked the cars first; the three hoods were cool to the touch. I scanned the lot for anything I might have missed and got back behind the wheel. I looped the building twice more searching the area for anything that might become a problem. There were no loitering men or suspicious vehicles anywhere within two blocks — until my car parked across the street from the front door.

It took just over three hours for me to spot what I had been waiting for. One man, in his late fifties, flanked by four younger men approaching the bar. No one spoke as they entered. They weren't friends — they were employer and employees. The old man was wearing a dark grey suit under an unbuttoned trench coat. His associates all wore black leather jackets. The styles varied, but they were all part of the standard bodyguard uniform. The men all had short haircuts and hard faces. None of them wore jeans. I figured the pleated dress pants were a sign that the bodyguards often had to follow the old man into nicer places than the Hammer and Sickle, and they knew enough to blend in. They didn't know enough to wear shoes that were made for work though. Their shoes were shiny leather, stylish; none appeared to have a strong toe or tread. Professionals never compromised functionality for appearance. They worried about the job first and how they looked second. Only lackeys cared if their shoes matched the occasion. One of the underlings held the door while another scanned the outside of the restaurant. I had my hand on the key in the ignition ready to move if I was made, but the scan passed over the car once, then twice.

The fact that none of the men noticed a car parked across the street as a threat confirmed what the shoes told me. The rabble moved into the restaurant, in a sloppy huddle, keeping the old man in the centre until the door was cleared.

The location, the clothes, and the poorly practised movements confirmed that the old man was a heavy in the Russian mob. He wasn't top shelf; the security was too sloppy, but he could have been a numbers man, an under-boss, or even a visiting associate from back home. I had never seen him in dealings I had with the Russians.

I started the car and drove around back of the restaurant to the still vacant space beside the Mercedes. I parked and put the keys in the front pocket of my jacket. I took off the seat belt and shifted so that I could get at the knife in my front pocket. The folding knife was a middle-of-the-market product with a four-inch blade and a sturdy locking mechanism. The handle was plastic with a raised grip that would resist prints. The blade would stay sharp for as long as I would need it, then it would sink in a sewer as deep as I needed it to.

I opened the knife and got out into the autumn air. I reversed the knife in my fist so that it could only be seen from behind me and used my free hand to ease the Volvo door shut. No one was walking by on the street as I moved to the side of the nearest German import. I hammered the knife into the rear tire, just above the rim, then moved to the other side and did the same before starting on the second and third cars. The slow leaks eased the cars gradually to the pavement; the movement was too subtle to set the car alarms off. I jogged around the building as the last of the air hissed from the tires. I opened the front door using my sleeve over my hand. My shoulder shoved the inner door open without suspicion. Without slowing down, I walked into the bar towards the tables.

Despite the city's smoking ban, the air was acrid with the scent of unfiltered European cigarettes. The clientele had shifted away from after-work drinkers to a more upscale type of clientele: the kind of upscale that still lived in the wrong part of downtown. The kind of people who could not get used to the quiet of the suburbs. The kind of people who drank hard alcohol in mob bars, dressed to the nines late on a Wednesday. At every table I passed, fair-skinned men and women with light hair were seated. Each face possessed the sharp features of Russia and the cold eyes of a hard people. The women were dressed stylishly, too stylishly for the bar — too stylishly for the city, and they were all far younger than the men they accompanied. Each young woman leaned into conversations with devotion, expressing interest in subtle nods and not-so-subtle displays of cleavage. The men all had the same dangerous expressions and the scars to verify them. The fancy rings and jewellery on hands, wrists, and ears fooled no one. They weren't bankers or lawyers — they were hoods who made good in the city.

Few faces turned from their dates to watch me walking by. My clothes were dull and nondescript, and they pulled no one's eyes to me. Anyone who did happen to look my way saw that I carried my own dangerous expression. There was no point trying to camouflage myself inside the Hammer and Sickle — the men inside could smell their own, and trying to mask what I was would only make me more conspicuous. To them I was just another grinder — they just had no idea who I grinded for.

I found the entrance to the kitchen behind the bar. One segment of the counter was raised to allow rear access, and the blond waitresses covering the tables used the space to move freely back and forth. My eyes glanced from the bar to the biggest group of people. My body followed my eyes, and I loped around two tables so that I approached the seated group of men head on. The old man I saw enter was in the centre of a corner booth. He was flanked by his men — well protected from contact with anyone in the bar. Anybody who wanted to speak with the old man would have to work through the layers of muscled insulation. I didn't want to talk with the old man. I let him see me coming. We locked eyes, and he gave me a hard stare. His look dissolved when he saw my face pull into a grin. Confusion cracked his ice-hard stare. Then I drew the police pistol and put a bullet in his chest.

The bodyguards did two things. The men directly to his left and right shielded themselves, while the men farther out lunged for the old man. They tried to climb over the cringing men to plug the red plume pumping out from under the old man's shirt. I pivoted and immersed myself in the pandemonium that had erupted. I had a few seconds to disappear before the bodyguards came to their senses and came after me. I threaded through the crowd and grabbed one of the waitresses. She probably thought me to be just an inconsiderate coward; I was no coward — I was just an inconsiderate man in need of a human shield. The sound of a curse coming from the waitress was deafened by the bark of a gun shot mingling with the cymbal crash of a bottle shattering behind the bar. I bent low and hustled behind the bar. I left the waitress blocking the doorway and ran into the kitchen as more bottles gave up their spirits to the air.

As soon as I rounded the first corner, I straightened and ran to the exit. The door was still closed — all of the kitchen staff stood frozen, staring at the doorway to the bar. I guessed shots weren't unheard of but probably unusual at such an early hour. I shouldered open the door and slid behind the wheel of the unlocked Volvo.

Inside the Volvo, I revved the engine and rolled down the window. I aimed the Glock out the window at the back door, resting my arm on the window sill. It took five seconds for the door to burst open and four bullets to send everyone back inside. I put the Volvo in reverse and screeched onto the street. I hooked backwards onto Sherman, shifting into drive while the car slid across the worn pavement. No shots came from the back of the restaurant, and no cars followed me as I raced away from the Hammer and Sickle.

I pulled into the first Tim Hortons I saw and parked out of sight from the road. I powered up the cell phone and called 911.

"There were shots fired at the Hammer and Sickle on Sherman. A man is dead. Please hurry. Oh, no!" I hung up the phone, powered it down, then walked into the coffee shop. I spent an hour eating muffins and drinking tea before I decided to turn on the phone again. I pulled out Detective Sergeant Huata Morrison's card and dialled his cell number.

"Morrison."

"It's me."

"You're late and I'm busy. But something tells me your tardiness and my working late are related."

"Where are you?"

"You know where I am, you fucker. I'm at the Hammer and Sickle." His voice turned into a harsh whisper for a moment. "A place I told you about. Some mobbed-up loser bit it, and guess what? None of the three employees who were working in the apparently empty bar here saw a thing."

"Sounds like you're in for a long night of detective work."

"Nah, I got a suspect. Just escaped from the hospital. I should be able to tie this up real easy."

"So you don't need any tips?"

"Tips?"

"You know, clues to help you solve the case."

"Nah, I don't need tips. I just need to have a talk with the bartender. Seems like he forgot to tell me about a suspicious customer who came in. Some joker with short hair and a beard."

"Sounds like leading a witness."

"An island boy like me does not know about such things, mate."

"That description won't match the ballistics," I said. My voice stayed monotone while my mouth turned up into a tight grin.

"Ballistics?"

"Yeah, that's my tip. I know that the crime was committed with a Glock police pistol. I even know where the gun can be found. Serial number is still on it too. No fingerprints though."

"You son of a bitch."

"How's your suspect list now?"

"You can't pull that shit on me. I'm a cop!"

"How long will that last when I tip the papers about the gun?"

There was a pause, then a sigh. "What do you want?"

"To stay a person of interest and to keep my prints and picture out of everything."

"That's impossible. There's a dead nurse in your hospital room. You're the prime suspect."

"Fix it," I said.

"I can't."

"You're acting like you have a choice. This is a new game. Now we're fishing in a boat together. You need to do some of that leading with a witness at the hospital."

"Leading to what?"

"Who's to say I wasn't a person of interest to more people than you?"

Morrison caught on. "So you were kidnapped. Probably already dead. Whoever killed that kid in the truck we found you near must have killed you too to keep you from talking."

"I stay dead and invisible, you stay Detective Sergeant."

"So we're partners. You got me and I got you."

"Looks that way."

"Can't be that way forever, mate. Something has to tip the scales eventually."

Morrison was right. No matter how crooked, he was still a cop, and no cop would put up with being pushed — they're too used to being the aggressors. There was no telling the amount of clout he had. He didn't fear bending the law to keep me from being printed or to get me out of the bed, so someone had to be on his side, someone big. Given enough time, he could spin the shooting at the club or fuck the ballistics reports. What I had on him only had a shelf life of a few days; then the scales would start to tilt in his favour again.

"Original deal then," I said. "I'll get you a fish, and you'll forget about me. Otherwise, I just cut bait and settle for taking you down with me."

There was no answer from the phone. I knew the cop was stuck where he didn't want to be. He was working with a crook instead of turning the screws. He was off balance. I had to keep him there because as long as he was uncomfortable, I had room to move.

"Give me a few days and I'll be in touch. I need one thing though," I said.

"What? Haven't I done enough for you?"

"I need info on a name."

The cop's voice became serious. He wanted me to lead him to something bigger. Any name I needed was something he could use to get ahead. I had to be careful about what I asked for — too much information could make me useless.

"What name?"

"Russian guy. I only got a first name: Igor. He's not street level. He's got enough clout to have that fat cop on payroll."

"I told you Miller's no rat. He's been my partner for years. I trust him with my life every day — he's solid."

"Solid like you? The CPR and the business card you gave me didn't seem by the books."

Morrison grumbled before hanging up, and I knew I'd hit a nerve. I swore under my breath into the dead connection. I had misread the cop. All this time I took him to be as bent as the rest of us, but I got it wrong. He was bent, but he didn't see it that way. In his mind, he was out for the greater good. He was a cop, and nothing he did was wrong because he was the law. Letting me out of the hospital was justifiable because it meant something worse would come in. Worse still, if Morrison thought he was a good cop, he would never really let me off — it would conflict with his own fucked-up logic. He would string me along until he achieved whatever goal he thought meted out justice, then he would turn on me. I was on the other side, and to a cop that meant I couldn't get away.

It had been years since I had met anyone who saw the world in sides. Simple logic made for dangerous people; they were easy enough to predict, but they brought chaos down all around them. Morrison had blinders on; he took an oath and wore a badge, and he figured everyone else felt the way he did about being a cop. He couldn't swallow the fact that one of his own people worked off the books for the Russians. He defended Miller twice when the evidence pointed to the contrary. That kind of myopia was like deep-seated racism; the kind that was bred into kids from the moment they took in air. His beliefs wouldn't wash away, and he would always be at their mercy. Morrison was blind and determined. He wouldn't forget about me, and he would trail that fat cop and the Russians along behind him until they could take their own shot. More people were going to get hurt before Morrison was done. I figured it was best that I was the one doing the hurting — I already had a head start.

CHAPTER SIX

The next morning, I went for breakfast at a Greek restaurant near the motel. Greece on King was too nice for the neighbourhood, and I took advantage before management clued in and decided to relocate. I slid into a booth that contained a discarded morning paper and leafed through the news. I was into the front-page story about a shootout at a local bar and the supposed links to the Russian mob, when a young woman approached the table. She was tall, about five-ten, with dark skin and dark hair. She wore little make-up and a black shirt and pants. The woman radiated beauty. I almost had to look away when she smiled and asked me if I was ready to order. I regained my composure, ordered steak and eggs, and got back to reading the paper. I didn't let my eyes wander to her ass as she walked away. I learned to shut out my pants long ago. It was always a fight, but I wouldn't let myself lose focus on a job.

I got to the end of the article, and twelve words floored me. I read them over and over again. The twelve words made me realize that I didn't need any help from Morrison to find Igor. The paper told me everything I needed to know: *The funeral will be at Thomas and Dunne on King and Wellington.* My feelings of stupidity for missing something so obvious were interrupted by the waitress pouring me a glass of ice water.

"You don't look happy," she said.

"I just realized I lost something."

"Not your wallet?" She looked concerned.

"No, not my wallet. The upper hand."

"Which glove is that? Left or right?"

The waitress waited for an answer, but I got back to reading the article — looking for anything I might have missed. The food came five minutes later with a side order of cold shoulder. I ate and thought about what I had said to Morrison. I asked him to find Igor. I gave no description, just the name and position of a man. It was possible that Morrison would be unable to put a face to the name right away. There might have been more than one powerful, mobbed-up Igor in the city, but it wasn't likely, and I knew it. All I could hope for was that the upcoming mob funeral would take precedence over everything else. Cops would be running security and surveillance to make sure they kept everything safe and on film. It would be a dangerous event despite the police presence. The cops would use the guise of security to plant themselves right outside the graveyard, and every Russian with a gun and a scar would be brazenly walking across the grass to the gravesite. Every member of the Russian mob, hopped up on anger and chemicals, would be daring the cops to touch them. Funerals were often places where wanted criminals had no problem showing their faces. The cops never touched them out of fear of the backlash from the rest of the made funeral attendees in front of the greedy camera

MIKE **KNOWLES**

lenses. I would have to join in the throng of media and police onlookers to find Igor and follow him home. I was on a cramped timetable, Morrison had a lead on me, and I had a lead on Igor. We all couldn't be in the lead forever.

I finished the steak and eggs, paid up, and checked out the waitress one last time. She caught me and flashed a glare that made it easier to look away. I nodded goodbye to the cook and left the restaurant with the newspaper under my arm.

I picked up the car from the motel parking lot and drove into the city, keeping an eye out for the kind of store I needed. The men's shop on Ottawa Street North wasn't a chain but a decades-old independently run business. The sign out front looked as though it had weathered a quarter of a century out on the street. I drove down the street looking for a place to park, only to be sent back the way I came. This part of Hamilton housed fabric and textile wholesalers. The clothing here would be plentiful and cheaper than anywhere else in the city. The tailor would also have put enough time in to have seen everything at least twice.

I finally found a spot in the parking lot of a retirement complex. As I walked to the men's shop up the street, I checked behind me to make sure I was clean. I didn't see a tail behind me, only an army surplus store. Something about the Ottawa Army Surplus registered in my mind. I had heard the name before from people in my line of work. I turned around and walked into the store.

An old bell announced my arrival, but there was no one around to notice. I walked the aisles looking at the peacoats and heavy work boots until I heard the shuffle of old feet. A grizzled man came out of the back room to meet me. He was the age that had no age. He could have been seventy as easily as he could have been ninety. Under a worn blue vest, he wore a faded red plaid flannel shirt and green pants pulled up to just below his nipples. Black suspenders locked the pants in place just in case they tried to make a break for it. The guy was too old to be working. He had to be some kind of serious broke to be behind a counter at his age. I knew I was in the right place; money would get me anything I needed. I just hoped the old man had the kind of anything I wanted.

"Sorry 'bout that, son. I was in the crapper."

"I understand," I said.

"Hell you do, boy! At my age, nature calls all the fucking time. Haven't been fishing with my buddies in years 'cause I have to piss so much. It's not natural."

I said nothing.

"Whachoo need?"

"I'm looking for holsters," I said.

"For what?"

"Two guns. A Glock and a small Smith and Wesson revolver."

"Where you want to carry these guns?"

"I need a shoulder rig for the Smith and Wesson, and a belt holster for the Glock."

"Who told you to come here?"

I didn't know the old man, or how far he crossed into the wrong side of the law, so asking about holsters was a good way to feel him out. His demand of a reference told me that I had asked the right guy. I played along. "Friend of a friend," I said.

The old man grumbled and walked through the doorway to the back room. When he turned, I caught sight of a hard hump under the back of his vest. Below the hump was another bump — one much more deadly.

MIKE KNOWLES

The old man came back a minute later with several shoulder rigs, a belt holster, and a metal case.

"Most of the shoulder rigs I got are too big for a small S and W. What barrel length are we talking about? Two inches?"

"Yeah."

"That's no good. You need something better?"

Igor's gun wasn't reliable, and I couldn't risk using the Glock again. "What do you have?" I asked.

The old man opened the case and turned it around on the counter so that I could see inside. Three guns were nestled into custom foam pockets. There were two fat black revolvers — a four-inch barrelled model 36 Smith and Wesson .38, and another Smith and Wesson .38, but this was the model 40. The other gun was a cheap Saturday Night Special. The guns were all bigger than Igor's small revolve, but none of them was in any condition that looked reliable.

As if sensing my thought, the old man spoke up. "They'll all fire. Tested them myself."

"What's behind your back?"

The old man frowned and harrumphed to himself. "What's behind my back?" He reached behind himself and strained to twist the gun out from under his vest. His bony, blue-veined hand came back holding a large black shape. The gun was heavy and ugly. There was no mistaking it.

"How much for the belt holster, that black shoulder rig there, and your Colt?"

"The .45 ain't for sale. It's mine. What's in that case there is all I got for you."

"Five hundred for the Colt and the two holsters," I said.

"Five hundred, hah! Thousand." And just like that, the Colt was on the market.

"Seven fifty and you hand it over with a spare magazine and a box of ammunition."

"Eight," he said.

"Done."

"Hee, hee, son, you made a fine purchase. Colt like that got me through Korea alive."

"Let me see it," I said, ignoring the mention of Korea. The old man wanted to sell the gun with a story; I had no time for old gun battles half a world away. I had my own gun battles a few streets over to deal with.

The old man stopped guffawing and got serious again. He slid out the magazine and passed me the gun.

I worked the slide and dry fired the gun. The trigger created an obscene snap like a loud "Fuck you." The gun was well oiled and in good condition.

"Wrap it up," I said.

The old man's humour returned at once, and he hustled behind the counter for a bag. He put the Colt in the shoulder rig and put everything in the bag. I peeled off the money and laid it on the counter. The old man snatched it faster than I would have bet he could move and laughed out loud.

"Pleasure doing business with you, son. And just so you know, the gun will have to be reported stolen. If you get caught with it, I'll call you a thief, and I'll press charges."

"I get caught with the gun no one will notice you. The gun will get swept under whatever rug they hide my body under."

The bell showed me out to the street, and I walked to the tailor. There was no bell to let anyone know I entered the men's shop. The sales floor was one large room lined with suits, shirts, pants, and ties. I walked along the racks inside the warm shop and smelled the pungent aroma of espresso being brewed. I spent a few minutes like that until I heard a man singing. The song wasn't in English — it

MIKE KNOWLES

was sung in a deep, rich Italian. The voice belonged to a man in his fifties with a full head of white hair who walked out from behind a curtain. His skin was olive, and his eyes had the type of puffy bags that sleep could never erase. He was dressed in an expensive black cashmere sweater and a pair of chocolate brown pants. His shoes were a shiny dark leather, and they went long past the toes into a narrow tip.

"*Buongiorno* — How can I help you?"

"I need a suit — light-weight, black, white shirt, and a tie. It will need to be tailored immediately."

My demands didn't faze the man. "*Bene, bene.* This can all be done. What suit you like?"

I found a middle-of-the-road suit and handed it over. He nodded at the suit and ushered me behind the curtain he came out of to a change room. Inside, I put on the shoulder rig and belt holster while I spoke through the door.

"You see the mob funeral coming up?"

"Russians, *pah*. They act like animals. They don't know how to behave like people. My family came to this country with nothing. My father scrimped and saved until he could buy us a house. Then he brought his sister and her children over and let them live with us. It was cramped, and some nights there was no food for the table, but he never once acted like those animals."

Through the door I replied, "But your people are no strangers to crime."

"You talking about the mafia? Some men went that way, yes, but not my father. Not my family. But even those who did, they never acted like those Russians. There was a code, there was honour. The mafia helped build this city; they helped protect immigrants who would have starved in the street. Immigrants less proud and less fortunate than my father. We are different."

I could have spent the better part of the day showing this man how every mob is the same. There's no honour. There's only a desire for money and power. Every mob kills for it — they bleed to keep it and cut to take it.

I kept my mouth shut and opened the door. I got what I wanted. I understood where the man stood.

"You look good in that suit, but the way it hangs. It's . . . it's . . . What is wrong there? Come here."

The man's hand felt the jacket. His touch was gentle as he felt over the fabric. He grunted when he felt the Colt in the shoulder harness.

"What's your name?" I asked.

"It's . . . my name is . . . I am Ottavio."

"Ottavio, I have a funeral to attend. The funeral of those Russian animals. I'm working under cover, and I want to blend in, so I need you to get rid of the bulge here, and here," I said pointing to the guns.

"You are police, eh? Oh my God, you had me worried. I thought you were Russian for a moment and you were going to kill me for what I said. Of course I will help you get those animals. Anything for the police. My *zio*, my uncle, was a police inspector back home in Palermo. He made my family very proud."

"So you understand how important it is that the suit fit well and that it conceals everything?"

"Of course, officer, the suit is no problem. It will hide everything." Ottavio winked when he said the word *everything*; his version of the word seemed more pleasant than mine. "I once tailored for a magician. No one ever saw where he kept his doves. Only I know his tricks, eh?"

The rest of the fitting went quickly. Ottavio made adjustments for an hour while I drank espresso and ate a few biscotti. I left a few hundred lighter, with the suit in a garment bag. I kept the Colt on, under the coat, close to my body.

wasted a day waiting for the funeral. I spent the entire time in the motel room watching local news, shitty daytime talk shows, and sitcoms. I ate greasy pizza and Diet Coke I bought nearby and waited.

The next day, dressed in my new suit carrying the new Colt and the revolver I took off Igor, I left for Dodsworth and Brown. I left the Glock inside a vent I managed to unscrew in the cramped motel bathroom. I couldn't risk having to fire it; the ballistics would ruin everything I had set up and create a window for Morrison to escape through. He could prove his gun was stolen and put me back on his leash.

The funeral home had a viewing from eleven to two. After that, the body was being laid to rest at a Russian church on Sanford, just down the street from the Russian hall Morrison told me about. St. Peter's Church was a large building housing a huge cemetery for the city's Russian population.

I parked three blocks away from Dodsworth and

Brown and waited. There were other nondescript cars waiting closer to the funeral home, and in them men sat with telephoto lenses pointed in the same direction. As long as I parked behind them, I wasn't in danger of getting on film.

I could barely make out the faces of the people going in and out of the funeral home, but it didn't matter — I was waiting for the drive to the cemetery. I spent three hours waiting. At 2:15, the long procession of high-end European cars began. From my spot, I saw inside each of the cars as they passed me. In the twelfth car, a bright yellow BMW, were Igor and Tatiana. Neither noticed me as they slowly passed. They sat silently in the car, smoking. No other yellow cars passed by with the procession — the rest were modestly coloured expensive vehicles. I waited for the line of cars to end, and for the three unmarked police cars to follow, before I drove to St. Peter's.

At the church, there were no spaces in front of the building at all. I did two drive-by's and saw none of the three unmarked police sedans that followed from the funeral home. I snaked through the nearby side streets for a few minutes until I came across the three cars. All three were abandoned, their engines still ticking. The cops would be trying to set up at the entrance and near the grave site so that they could get clear head shots of everyone coming and going. I drove two streets over and parked in a court that had a footpath leading towards the church. The path was wide enough to drive through, and I parked the car in a spot on the road that would allow me access to both the street and the path. If I had to leave fast, I wanted options. I jogged back to the three unmarked cars two blocks over. I looked around and saw no one on the streets. My hand went inside my jacket and came out with the folding knife. I put the blade into six passenger side

MIKE KNOWLES

tires. Not even the squirrels turned their heads to look at the quiet hissing I left behind as I walked away.

I headed back to the church and scanned the street corners. I found the first cop two streets up with his lens pointed towards the church entrance. Outside the entrance, eight men and two women stood, all smoking in the sunlight. If they noticed the cop, they never let on. I stayed on the opposite side of the street, away from the lens, as I walked past the church. Around the corner, I spotted Igor's yellow BMW. The car looked to run about sixty grand — forty if you tried to re-sell it yellow. It was a vehicle that screamed, "Look at me! I have money and fine things, but they're useless unless you look at me."

I passed the car and walked down the road. Each driveway had a car or two parked in it. I had to pass four Japanese imports before I found an empty driveway. I followed the brick path to the backyard, where a wooden fence separated it from the church property. Through the slats, I watched the cemetery and a long procession of men and women walking behind a casket. I put my hands on top of the fence and hoisted myself over. No one noticed me landing inside the cemetery grounds — all eyes were on the casket. I quickly made my way to a large tombstone and bent, pretending to clean off the dirt and debris on the stone. There were still two cops somewhere with cameras, and I would be in their sights unless I was careful. The cops wouldn't be allowed inside the church grounds; the funeral was private, and that meant the law too. They would have to find a spot somewhere nearby that offered a good view of the funeral. I scanned the trees on the other side of the cemetery until I saw a beam of light reflect off glass in the foliage. Inside the dense trees one of the cops was getting a great straight shot of the whole guest list.

I kept my head low and walked along the property line

away from the funeral. I moved off the lawn and into the trees of the small forest bordering the cemetery, following a path probably formed by the feet of hikers and kids on their way to bush parties. Back in the trees, I made my way around to the spot where I'd seen the glint of the lens. I had to go slowly to avoid making any noise; the ground was littered with beer bottle and pop can landmines. It took five minutes to work my way to the photographer I had noticed. The police paparazzo was in front of an old fire pit standing with a large camera to his face. He didn't know I was behind him until the .45 pressed into his neck.

"Put the camera down," I said.

"I'm a cop, asshole."

"Put it down, now."

"Are you fucking crazy? I'm a cop."

I pushed the .45 hard into his neck, forcing him to bend. Instinctively, both his hands held on to his camera to protect it from falling to the ground. My left arm jerked back, then drove forward into the cop's side. The blow was sudden, and I timed it to the cop's exhale. He had no way to protect himself from the sudden impact. I heard a crack like a pop from a campfire and then a sharp intake of breath before the cop dropped his camera and fell to his knees. No one in the funeral procession one hundred metres away looked towards us. I pulled the cop's gun and threw it into the forest, then holstered the .45 and freed the cuffs from the cop's belt. The cop offered little resistance while I shackled his hands behind his back. He lay gasping, trying to get his wind back, while I clicked through the stored pictures in the digital camera. There were a couple hundred shots, but I moved through them fast. I saw a shot of a yellow BMW and deleted it. I got rid of another few close-ups of Igor too. The new stitches on his face from where I yanked his cheek open made him easy to spot.

MIKE KNOWLES

When I was through all of the shots, I sat up the cop, who had managed to start breathing normally again.

"What's your name?"

"Broke my ribs, you fucker."

"Cracked maybe, but not broke. Name?"

"Bill."

"All right, Bill. I need to know a few things, then I'm gone. No one will ever have to know about this. You do it fast, and you can get shots of the rest of the funeral."

"I'm gonna find you, and I'm gonna . . . Hey! What are you doing?"

"Erasing your work. Tough to explain why you came back with nothing to the brass. Might get you bumped off this little task force. Maybe put back in a car on nights."

"Stop, stop." Bill was whining.

"You going to play ball?"

"Fine, fine, what do you want?"

"I'm going to click back through the shots. You tell me who's who. Names, rank, territory, everything."

"I don't know everybody."

I turned the camera and took five rapid shots of the cop cuffed in the dirt.

"Hey, what are you doing? Stop that!"

"I'm gonna hand this off to one of the other cops and let them deal with you. You'll be a real hero."

"Shit, don't do that."

"Then stop jerking me around. You're not working the entrance. You're set up to get shots of the big players. They don't give that job to someone who doesn't know all the faces."

"All right, all right. I'll do it."

I clicked through each frame and listened to Bill tell me who was who. There were a lot of faces, and I asked about each. I didn't care about any of them, but I didn't want Bill to know that. When Bill assigned Sergei's name to a picture of a man at the front of the procession, I listened closely.

"That's the man in charge, Sergei Vidal. He runs the whole Russian mob in Hamilton and Niagara."

"Why Niagara?"

"The casinos and the circus. He uses the Russian circus to get his people into the country. The casinos are the next step; they're already full of crime and money — Sergei used the Russian imports to muscle his way in, then to keep what he took. It only took a few years for the Russians to become major players. The other gangs just couldn't stop them; it's impossible to put fear into the Russians. They've all made their bones under some of the meanest gangsters in the world, and most have done time inside prisons that make puppy mills look like a Hilton. The Russians make a killing off the casinos and use the circus to launder the proceeds. It's a good system. The books are easily fudged, and everyone in the circus is on the payroll, or their family back home is used as blackmail."

"Who guards him?"

"Always five or more men."

"But who guards him? Used to be a big guy, Ivan, but he's gone. Who took his place?"

"Those two on either side of him are his personal security. They're former Russian military. Served in Afghanistan and Chechnya."

"Names?"

"Nikolai and Pietro. Nick and Pete to everyone. I don't know their last names, too many V's and backwards letters. Mean motherfuckers. They killed four Cambodian kids last year when they took a run at Sergei in a nightclub. The kids used machetes and tried to swarm him. They ended up cut to pieces themselves. No witnesses of course, only stories."

We went through thirty more shots until we got to the cars. I asked detailed questions about everyone who seemed important so that Bill would have no insight into what I was really after.

"Where is the third camera?"

"What?"

"I saw one out front, you in the trees, where is number three?"

Bill was over caring about betrayal. "Parking lot," he said.

"Keys are behind your back, Bill, your gun is ten metres that way," I said, pointing in the wrong direction.

Bill began fumbling behind his back while I walked away down the path. He grunted as he lost his balance and rolled over onto his side. I heard him gasp and swear under his breath as his damaged ribs made contact with the ground.

I left the trees and climbed the fence without looking behind me. I came down over the fence without anyone watching from the funeral procession.

"Nice suit."

Shit, I thought. I turned, already shrugging my shoulders, as Morrison's meaty fist collided with my head. I shrugged enough to take most of the blow with my shoulder and trapezius muscles. I brought my hands up, but a second punch never came my way. Morrison closed the distance between us in two steps and took the lapels of my coat in both hands. In a fraction of a second, he pivoted below me and used his hips to get me airborne. I felt his back, like a heavy tree stump, rise, lift me, and throw me. I landed three feet away from the beefy cop. The wind was out of me, but I had been there before. I saw his feet approaching and rolled off my stomach onto my side, my hands already reaching for the foot I knew was coming. Morrison took a big soccer kick at my ribs, but it never connected. My hand blocked the kick, and I rolled away. I put my hands out again, ready to block another kick, but it didn't come. Morrison dove onto my back and looped an arm around my neck. Instinctively, my jaw pressed into my chest, protecting my windpipe from his forearm.

"Back home, I was a national champ in judo, mate." His breath was hot in my ear. "I've twisted bigger and better than you. Only this time, there's no ref to make me let you go."

Most people fight a choke in a blind panic. They strain at the threat — pulling at whatever obstructs the airway. Not me, I learned all about chokes in my teens.

As soon as my uncle took me under his wing, I never had a moment's rest. If my back was to my uncle or my guard was down, he was on me. It didn't matter what the task was; doing dishes, taking out the trash, even brushing my teeth might be met with a barrage of sneak attacks.

One August morning, my uncle came into the kitchen arms full. He was carrying a load of dry cleaning he said was for a job, and he stumbled over a chair I left pulled out. I cringed at my stupidity, knowing I would pay for it, and bent to pick up the clothes. A plastic dry cleaning bag went over my head as I came up with my arms full. I could see the blurred kitchen through the bag as I groped for the counter to hold myself upright. My uncle pulled me to him, with two hands, as the bag fogged with more and more hot air and spit. After thirty seconds, I gave up on the counter and pulled at the hands around my neck. I was exhausted and panting as panic set in. I went to my knees, scratching at the hands, but the clear prison never let up. Blackness took me seconds later.

MIKE KNOWLES

I woke up on the floor to find the dry cleaning gone. My uncle sat at the table, expressionless in his chair, eating cantaloupe.

"You still ain't ready, boy."

I coughed and sucked air deep into my strained lungs. "Bag was a dirty trick."

"Oh, you think so? You think there's a fucking rule book out there? You think there's a penalty box for people? Forget that shit and tell me what just happened."

"You choked me out," I said.

"Tell me what you did about it."

"I tried to stay on my feet. Then I tried to get your hands off my neck. You were too strong, and I ran out of air."

"Why didn't you tear open the bag?"

I sat there dumbfounded.

"It's a plastic bag. You could have opened it with your finger. Why did you care about the counter or my hands?"

"I . . . I . . ."

"CIA uses clear bags. People tear open black ones, but the clear ones — no one touches those. It's psychological, I suppose. You panic and your mind goes into a primal sort of thinking. You can see through the bag, so your brain doesn't register it; it focuses on the hands and body first. That shit doesn't matter though. Dead is dead no matter what your mind-set. You have to think clearest when you're dying. That's when you have to keep your head, or else someone else is going to take it. What good is thinking if you forget it when you need it most? School's out for today. Get to the gym."

I walked out with my head low, the lesson burning in my cheeks. There were other tests after that, but I never lost my head again. I stayed calm when I needed to, and I stayed conscious — most of the time.

Morrison's forearm worked under my jaw. He rotated the bone back and forth using his whole body to pull his limb against my windpipe. I ignored the pain, and the arm, choosing instead to dig a thumb into his eye. He screamed in pain, and the hold loosened a fraction. My other hand found his balls, and I squeezed hard. The choke came loose, and I rolled away. I was on my feet before he was; Morrison wasn't using his hands to stand — they were holding his face and his crotch as he tried to get up. He saw me coming, and he covered up as I had, but I circled around his guard and pounded a kick into the base of his spine. He yelped, and his hands left his front in favour of his back as the impact shot up my leg. I saw his eyes focus through the pain and knew he wasn't done. We both drew on each other at the same time.

"Noise isn't what you want," I said.

"Fuck you. You don't know what I want," Morrison said as he got to his feet one shaky foot at a time. In his fist, he held a snub-nosed revolver.

"Using your drop piece?" I asked.

"Seem to have misplaced my service issue. Where'd you pick up the .45?"

"Yard sale. Why are you here?"

"I'm here to see the players. I love it when shit doesn't go their way. I had to take a personal day just to get here."

"You let them see you?"

"Nah, I'm not suicidal, mate. Rubbing it in is bad business. I'd end up on the business end of a drive-by if I rubbed it in at a funeral."

"So you saw me and . . . What the fuck happened to your eyebrows?"

"Fucking tape you put on my head took off my eyebrows. I had to fill 'em in with a make-up pencil. It's big laughs at the station."

I chuckled, but the gun never shook. "So you saw me, and you figured it was payback time?"

"That's right, fuckwit."

"You'll just be a dead cop next to a cemetery full of suspects."

"Not if I shoot you first."

"Then you're an off-duty cop using his drop piece on his personal day next to a cemetery full of police cameras and Russian gangsters. How many questions would come out of that?"

Morrison thought about it.

"Climb back over the fence and watch the rest of the show. You can see everything fine from behind the tombstones. You stay here, it's gonna get loud," I said, dusting off my suit with one hand; the other kept the .45 aimed at centre mass.

"We ain't done, mate. We're gonna settle up somewhere private. Just you and me."

"It's hard to look threatening when your eyebrows can't furrow."

He took a step towards me, but I waved him away with the .45. "Go, funeral is about to end, and neither of us wants to be here when that happens."

Morrison slid over the fence quicker and quieter than I thought a man his size ever could, making me think the judo claim was no joke. I'd spent so much time trying to figure out what Morrison wanted from me that I'd underestimated him. He might have been a little crooked, but he was more than a bruiser. He was a good cop. I never saw him watching me in the cemetery. He got through my radar and almost crushed my throat. I had to remember that even off balance Morrison was no slouch. As soon as he disappeared, I jogged out of the yard, crossed the street, and went through two backyards before I set foot on the street. I was far enough down the road to make the church hard to see. But that meant it was hard to see me from the church. I found the court where I had parked my car and slid behind the wheel. I drove over to the street where Igor's yellow BMW was, backed into an empty driveway on the opposite side of the street, and waited.

The cars on the street began moving fifteen minutes after I parked the Volvo. Igor's yellow eyesore stayed put for another twenty minutes. His car was the second to last left on the street when he came sauntering around the corner. Tatiana followed in his wake — stumbling every fourth or fifth step. The way he let her trail behind told me that seeing her like this wasn't new. She stumbled coming out of another stumble and turned her ankle. Tatiana went sideways into a bush just as Igor unlocked the car with his key fob. He stamped his foot, marched back to her, and yanked her out of the shrub. He slapped her with his left palm and dragged her by her left bicep to the car. One of her feet kept rolling off its sole and dragging sideways on the pavement as he pulled her. She didn't seem to notice the pain, and Igor didn't notice, or care about, the extra drag. He pushed her against the rear door and held her up against the car with his hip while he opened the passenger side. She laughed and said something to him before he shoved her ass first into the car. He bent and crammed her feet inside before slamming the door. Igor ran a hand through his hair and looked around for witnesses before walking around to the driver side. On the curb, half in the gutter, lay the shoe Tatiana had been dragging sideways on the pavement.

The engine of the yellow car started, and I watched Tatiana's window roll down. Her hand came out holding a cigarette until the car screeched ahead and she had to sacrifice it for a steadying hold on the window sill. I started the Volvo and rolled after the BMW.

Igor drove like an asshole — too fast on residential streets and hooking in and out without signalling on busier roadways. All he achieved was getting to the stop-lights faster than anyone else. I stayed far back and let him blaze a trail, knowing there was no way I was going to lose sight of that bright yellow car.

We raced into the core of the city and joined King Street. Igor bobbed and weaved until he screeched his tires onto Bay Street North. The street had cars parked on both sides, leaving only one lane for through traffic. Igor raced down the centre lane, forcing oncoming traffic to swerve into vacant parking spaces for cover from the yellow blur flying at them. Igor put some distance between us while the honking motorists pulled out of their temporary hiding places. I waited for my turn to use the street and then sprinted, pedal to the floor, down the pavement. The Volvo reacted fast, and the power of the engine surprised me. The souped-up machinery under the battered hood came to life like a waking animal — its guttural growl turned into a roar — and went zero to sixty in a few seconds. I caught up to Igor fast, and I had to slam on the brakes to avoid getting too close. He had slowed from his breakneck speed to turn into a driveway. I pulled to the curb twenty metres away and watched Igor once again drag Tatiana. She fell onto the driveway, not being able to keep up with only one high heel on. Igor used her arm and hair to get her vertical and kept his grip to get her the rest of the way into the house. He dragged her inside and slammed the door. I left the curb and turned the corner without looking back at yet another abandoned high heel, this time on the doorstep.

CHAPTER EIGHT

B ayfront Park was across the street from Igor's house. From a parking lot behind a seasonal ice cream shop, I could see his yellow car in the driveway. The ice cream shop had probably closed a few months ago after the kids went back to school. Most of the graffiti on the back of the small shack was new and done in a variety of mediums. Gang signs and love notes were temporarily etched in paint and marker all over the wall. The spot was a good choice because I wouldn't have to worry about a cop checking on the car — joggers used the Bayfront all the time, so there were always a lot of cars parked nearby. It was 4 p.m., and I had no idea how long I was going to have to wait for Igor to come out of his house. I figured I had some time and pulled out of the lot. I drove into the city, found a Middle Eastern restaurant that advertised shwarma, and went inside.

The restaurant was dark, and the walls were without decoration. There were no tables, only booths lined with a dark maroon vinyl. One booth at the back was loaded with kids. A white kid, a black kid, a Filipino, and an Arab sat yelling loud jeers and obscenities to each other across the tight booth.

"I own you in Runescape. I pawn you like a noob every time."

"Sure, sure, George. That's why I sold my points to Matthew for fifty bucks. You suck, George."

I knew they were speaking English, but I had no idea what was being said. I walked past them and smiled at the woman behind the counter. She looked at the kids and rolled her eyes.

"What do you want today?"

"What do you eat?"

"Pardon?"

"What do you eat when you eat here?"

"Oh, I get the shwarma dinner with the garlic and hot sauce."

"Give me two and an iced tea."

The woman got to work filling Styrofoam containers with salad, rice, and chicken. She then topped the meat and rice with two heavy sauces. The kids quieted as two of them broke from the pack and stood in line behind me. They gave me tough stares when I looked in their direction, and I resisted the urge to show them the butt of the .45.

"Do you like Runescape?" the blond kid with braces and a sideways hat asked. He laughed to his friend as soon as he asked the question, thinking he was embarrassing me.

"What do you want?" the girl behind the counter demanded to know from the boy.

"Could I have a can of Mountain Dew?"

"Go sit down and leave my customers alone. I'll bring it to you when I'm done."

The girl finished my order and took my cash.

MIKE KNOWLES

"Where's my Mountain Dew?" the blond kid asked again the second the money touched the till.

The girl sighed and turned, leaving the till open, to get a can from the lowest rack of the fridge. She banged her head on the open drawer as she stood, and the boys all laughed at her. She followed me out on her way to the boys' table. I left to the sound of the boys asking her if she liked whatever Runescape was. My .45 stayed in my jacket, and no one watched me leave.

Outside, I put the food on the floor of the back seat, where it would be held in place by the small space on the floor behind the driver's seat. I looked back at the restaurant, through the window at the kids, and ground my teeth. Being forced to work for Morrison made watching the bullies impossible. The big cop was using me just like the kids were using the girl behind the counter. I needed an outlet — something to release the pressure before it came out all on its own. It was then that I noticed the bikes leaning against the wall just below the window. No one else was visible in the lot, so the bikes must have brought the four assholes to the restaurant. They weren't locked up, just left in view from the window. I got in the Volvo, adjusted the mirror, and put the car in reverse. With a sudden bump, the car backed over the curb. There was a metallic crunch and then grinding as the bikes compressed under the old steel bumper of the Volvo. The bumper was worn and dented, so I didn't worry about any new dings standing out. I shifted back into drive and left the lot as the kids from inside ran out to stare at their bikes. I was around the corner too fast for my plates to be seen and lost in traffic before they could call anyone to complain.

I drove back out to Bay Street North and parked behind the ice cream shack again. The yellow BMW was still there. I spent an hour eating and waiting until I had to piss. I dumped what was left of the iced tea and used the bottle. I wasn't leaving again without Igor, so the bottle was the only option.

At 6:30, Igor left the house and started the BMW. Tatiana stayed inside, and her shoe stayed on the porch. Igor tore out of the driveway and headed towards downtown using Barton Street East.

He changed lanes every few seconds and kept the car a few kilometres over eighty the whole way. I pushed through traffic relying on the red lights and the colour of the car to keep him in sight. Ten minutes later, he turned a quick right on Mary Street and parked the car in a lot behind a commercial property. The spot he took was near the rear exits, and it had a sign above it that I couldn't make out from the street. I kept going, then turned onto a side street where Igor wouldn't see me turn around. When I looped back onto Mary Street, Igor was walking to Barton. I crept up the street with my lights off, watching him cross the street and go left at the corner. I gave him a few seconds before I pulled the car to the intersection. I watched until he turned into a doorway of a strip club. The Steel City Lounge was a low-end joint that catered to the off-duty prison guards from the nearby Hamilton Detention Centre. I swung my head right and looked at the detention centre a couple hundred metres down the street and knew it was looking back at me. The building was like a predatory beast always on the prowl. The Barton Jail was a maximum security facility that held the worst and the dumbest. I flipped off the building from the car, checked the rear-view, and reversed back down the street to a curbside parking space.

I pulled the keys from the ignition and followed Igor's trail to the Steel City Lounge. I passed the building, looking inside the open entrance. If there were bouncers frisking anyone, I would have to put the guns back in the car. What I saw made me happy. There was no cover, no dress code, and a sign proclaiming that everyone was welcome.

I walked around the block looking at the side and rear fire exits and at the fence surrounding the parking lot behind the property where Igor had parked. There were several holes in the perimeter of the fence and one portion around back that was almost falling down. It looked as though a car had backed into the fence and no one had bothered to fix it up.

When I came back around, I loosened my tie and walked right inside. I wasn't at all worried about being spotted. I had been invisible for over a decade. As a teen, my first lessons in invisibility started early. Invisibility was a necessity. Until I learned to blend in, I had been barraged with questions about why I was out of school.

At first, I just didn't look people in the eye; it warded some people off, but it didn't make me invisible. The hard men and women my uncle associated with just shoved me and demanded to know why I wasn't where I should have been. It wasn't that they were concerned about my education; they could give a shit about the three R's. They knew that a kid hanging around attracted attention. Someone else would want to know the same thing they did, and if I didn't have an answer, any job I was on would be spoiled like milk left in the sun. At first, I tried to tough my way around my inquisitors, once going so far as to tell a safe man to fuck off when he questioned me. He didn't respond, he just looked at my uncle and then knocked me out — chipping a tooth in the process.

That night, while I sat with a bag of frozen peas on my jaw, my uncle asked about my mouth. I told him it was all right because of the peas, and he assured me that it was as sure as fuck not. He said it was too saucy for such a green

93

kid. I told him about the question and how I thought going on the offensive would make it go away. My uncle laughed. "You can't be mean every time. That will usually just bring on whole other sets of questions. You can't let them see you, boy."

"You mean stay in the car?"

"You can't always stay in the car. You have to be able to walk around in plain sight. What I'm talking about is being invisible in front of everyone's eyes. You have to learn to be a ghost, and not like Casper. I mean fucking gone."

"How?"

"It's all in your head. But you won't believe me until I show you. Get your coat."

We drove to west Hamilton and parked in a lot that housed a variety store, a fish and chips restaurant, and a pool hall. We walked down the steps to the pool hall, and my sinuses were all at once struck with the smell of dirt, smoke, and spilt beer. My uncle took a deep breath and exhaled slowly. He put an arm around me and pointed to a row of pinball machines and video games.

"These here are mob-owned, boy. I once saw a local tough guy put a pool cue through one. Next day, a leg breaker shows up to cart away the machine and to find the guy that broke it."

"What happened to the guy?" I asked.

"Darndest thing, the truck that was hauling the machine away hit him in the street." My uncle laughed as though he had just heard a particularly funny joke instead of a tale of street justice. "Here's ten bucks. Have some fun."

I forgot about being invisible and spent an hour play-ing Golden Axe. There were three characters to choose from, a big Conan-looking guy all muscle and sword, a beautiful warrior woman with a sword and implants, and a dwarf with a big axe. I chose the dwarf with the axe because hardly anyone ever picked the dwarf. The game had spent years killing the barbarian or the broad, maiming their digital good looks long into the night. In my mind, everyone was scanning for the next buff hero — no one would see the dwarf coming until the big axe spoke up and said hello in its brutal language. Time flew by, and on the hour my uncle put his heavy hand on the back of my neck. His fingers dug hard into muscle and nerves as he spoke in my ear. "Lesson's not over, boy. You've been here an hour, what's the guy behind the counter look like?"

I instinctively tried to turn my head, but the calloused mitt on my neck wouldn't let me.

"Speak up. What's he look like?"

"I don't know."

"Why not?"

"I didn't look at him. I was busy."

"Son of a bitch might as well have been invisible, eh? That's the first trick. When you don't want to be seen, you have to be where the person's interest ain't. The guy behind the counter pulled it off without trying because you're young and stupid, but there's a science to it. You have to notice everything around you. Take in everything that happens and everything that don't. You want to be unseen, you move when other things happen. You pick your spots. You can be nowhere in plain sight as long as you feel what's around you. You move with the room, and it's like you're not even there. Understand?"

I nodded my head as much as the hand on my neck would allow, but my uncle wasn't finished.

"It's different when you're in a room with one or two people. Then you're part of the room because you're a focal point. There's nowhere to hide in the spotlight. You sit quiet in that spotlight long enough people feel like they have to say something to fill the void. And our kind of people don't know anything polite. If you make them wonder, they're gonna dig at you until they find something they understand. Only your words will make you invisible. You got to make people uncomfortable, make them want to look somewhere else. And I'm not talking about the 'Fuck you' shit you tried. When you want to stay invisible, you have to use remarks that put people on the defence. Put something mean and uncomfortable out there, then fade back. People will be glad to ignore you then. But what you put out comes from observation. You have to watch how people talk, how they stand, what they look at. You need to find something that will rattle them in the few moments you have, then you go at it with precision, not brute force. If you put out anything that sounds like a challenge, everyone will get your scent. A challenge is primal. Every animal recognizes it and instinctively pays attention to it. You challenge someone in our world everyone will see you, because they'll be trying to put your lights out. Understand?"

It was a week before someone else on the job asked me why I wasn't in school. I had studied hard, and I was ready. "I thought you said this guy was a pro, Uncle Rick. You sure this is the guy we need to see?"

There was silence in the room until my uncle spoke. "Are you?"

"Yeah, yeah, sure, Rick. I was just making conversation. Let's get down to business."

No one spoke to me again that whole afternoon. No one even looked my way even though I was three feet away from the conversation the entire time. When no one was looking, my uncle rubbed my head. Rare praise from the man who raised me to become a ghost.

That night, my uncle took me to one of the big box

electronic stores in Ancaster. On the way in he said, "What you did today was good. Now I want to see if you can move with the room. Each of these minimum wagers inside here works on commission. They're hungrier than sharks and less decent. I'm gonna move around the store for fifteen minutes, and you're gonna come with me. If we get stopped, it won't be because of me. It'll be because you couldn't flow with the environment. Don't screw up, boy. Understand?"

We spent twenty minutes in the store. The last five were spent moving within feet of the bored employees. I moved with my uncle for a while, until he seamlessly shifted behind me and began following me. The automatic doors were the only thing to recognize our departure. There was no head rubbing this time — only a small compliment and a big criticism.

"You might have a knack for this, but you almost screwed up. You looked at the girl in the music section, and she saw you. The employee there picked up on her distraction, and he almost followed it to you. You don't shut off your dick, you don't vanish. Understand?"

I nodded and got in the car.

The Steel City Lounge advertised thirty dancers, but I counted only twenty on rotation for the dinner crowd. The seats in front of the long stage were full of beefy looking men with short haircuts and faded tattoos. Each seemed comfortable with the close proximity of the man beside him, making me think that they were guards from the jail winding down after a long shift. The girls were the opposite of everything they looked at all day, and they watched with a carnivorous interest.

I took a corner seat and scanned the room. Igor wasn't on the bottom floor — he was in the second floor VIP area talking to a topless waitress and playing it cool, judging by the look on his face. Around him were four pale men in dark suits and sunglasses. They spoke to random girls who weren't talking to Igor and kept their eyes on him at all times. Igor said something over the head of the owner of the tits he was looking at, and all the men laughed loudly enough for me to hear them over the music. The attention and fake laughter meant Igor was important to them.

The strip club looked to be Igor's haunt. It was clear he was the man in charge from his free movement in the VIP lounge and the number of cold-looking sycophants he garnered. How much business went down in the club was up in the air. Igor claimed to be doing what a neighbourhood boss named Mikhail did before him. I figured that meant he collected money from all of the blood-stained hands of the mob in the area and passed the dirty currency on to his boss, Sergei Vidal. Igor wasn't enough to get Morrison off me, but he knew who I was, so whatever went down had to include him. I had to find out what Igor was into and how it got back to his boss, because Sergei was no fish — he was a whale, and he'd definitely get me off the hook.

CHAPTER NINE

I sat in the strip club for six hours. I steadily ordered drinks from the waitresses and poured them on the floor a bit at a time. The carpet under my feet was dark and industrial grade; it was probably used to getting wet, and it hid my drinks just fine. I tipped well enough to stay seated but not well enough to get any company. The club was full of plenty of other men looking for an eyeful and more than willing to pay for a handful. The girls almost instinctively avoided me. They knew which men had money to spend like bees knew which flowers had pollen.

Igor was big man on campus in the Steel City Lounge. People showed up with heavy duffel bags over their shoulders and left with them empty under their arms or crumpled in their fists. Whatever was in the bags never came down the stairs — there had to be a safe upstairs in the VIP lounge.

Loud thunderous music pounded out of the speakers and moved my glass across the table a millimetre at a time whenever it was empty. I was seen, but never noticed, not even by the waitress. I was part of her route. She brought me a new drink when she came by like a robot. No one else looked my way — I was in a pocket between the action. On one side, the stage dazzled lonely men with lights and implants. On the other, the bar hummed with customers ordering food and drinks. Igor never looked down unless it was to order one of the stage performers up to his lounge at the end of her set. When the dancers began to leave, and not get replaced by another Stepford whore, I realized how long I had been in the club and the toll the time took on my bladder. I took in the room and waited for my spot. I had to wait for the room to cough so I could move in the space provided by the spasm. I moved when a drunken customer got handsy with a girl and a bouncer had to deal with him. No one's eyes followed me; they were all glued to the beating. I was part of the room, the background no one pays attention to, just like my uncle had taught me to be.

The bathroom was disgusting and empty, but I used it all the same. I took my time drying my hands, timing my exit. I left the bathroom in tune with a loud entrance of another girl from the speakers. I waited outside the bathroom for the peeler to hit the audience with a tease. Within a few seconds, both of her clear heels left the stage as she slid upside down on the pole towards the floor. Men hooted and hollered as I moved under the VIP stairs and out the door.

I pulled the car out front and killed the engine. I let the back window down to avoid clouding the windows and waited for Igor.

One by one, drunks stumbled out empty handed and alone. Igor left, unaccompanied, at 3 a.m. with nothing more than what he showed up with. He got in his car and peeled away.

MIKE KNOWLES

I didn't follow. Instead, I waited outside. I wanted to see if he left moving the contents of whatever was in those duffel bags to one of his guys. I saw three of the VIP's leave together, but none of them carried a thing. I got out of the car and followed them on foot down the street. Like Igor, they'd parked in the lot behind the strip club. They were loud and boisterous as they walked around the building. They didn't turn their heads once to see me two metres behind them. I let my footsteps fall in the same tempo as theirs, and I slowed my breathing down. I moved closer and put my hand on the butt of the .45. It would have been easy to put a bullet into each of the three men. I was so close I could do it before any of them turned around to see who it was that was killing them. It was clear that Igor didn't work with pros; he had men on staff who were sloppy like he was. They were probably childhood friends or the only people who didn't laugh at him. I stopped following when the three men turned off the sidewalk and stepped into the lot behind the building. I had learned enough about Igor's business and the help for one night.

I got back behind the wheel and watched the rest of the employees leave. No one left with anything larger than a purse. When the windows went dark, I drove out to Igor's house on Bay Street and made sure the yellow car was there — it was. I drove back to the motel for a couple hours of sleep and was back behind the empty ice cream shack at 6 a.m. with a bagel in hand. I ate, drank, and pissed in a bottle in the car until 2:30. Then I followed Igor to a salon to watch him get his hair cut and his nails done. He went from the salon to Limeridge Mall, where he bought shirts and pants at Urban Behaviour while I watched him and pretended to shop at a nearby HMV.

Igor was back home at five. I noticed that someone had picked up Tatiana's shoe while we were gone. I left the car behind the vacant building and jogged across the street. The blinds in the windows were all turned. No one saw me as I ran down the driveway, past the yellow car, to the side of the house. The side of the house was all brick, and there were only two doors to be found. One leading to the garage, the other into the house. Neither door was unlocked, and both seemed to have a handle lock as well as a deadbolt. I moved around the back of the house, where a deck sat below a long row of kitchen windows. There was no way to pass unseen to the other side of the house, so I retraced my steps and crept around the front of the house to the other side.

On the other side, I found a basement window unlocked and screenless. I crouched and examined the dimensions of the window. I figured I could wiggle my way through the small space with little trouble. Around the corner to the backyard, I found myself on the other side of the deck below a kitchen window; it was up, and I could hear voices coming from inside the house.

"How could I take you to the salon? I told you I had a 2:45 appointment. You don't get up till 4:30!" Igor was screaming in heavily accented English.

"You could've woken me up!" Tatiana slurred when she spoke, but she seemed to be holding her own in the loud conversation.

"Do I look like a fucking alarm clock? I am the one who makes the money, I put food on the table, now I am to wake you up too? *Nyet.* Do you clean? *Nyet.* Do you sleep all day and get high? *Da!* That's what you do!"

"Maybe it's because I am bored. You don't take me out. You don't talk to me. If you could get it up, at least you could fuck me."

There were loud stomps building in intensity and force. "What did you just say to me?" Igor demanded to know.

"Igor, I . . . I . . . I am sorry, Igor. I didn't mean it. Please don't!"

Sounds of domestic violence trickled down through the window into the backyard.

"I am a man, you treat a man like a king, you junkie! Clean my house and clean yourself up. You talk that way to me because of the shit you put in your arm. You're high already. You're lucky I don't cut it out of you."

It was only 5:00. Tatiana had only been up thirty minutes, by Igor's clock, and she was already in the early stages of being high. It was a regular thing, judging from the similar state she was in at the funeral. Tatiana was sobbing loudly between the slaps and crashes.

"You want to be my wife and you act like this? How can I marry a junkie? You were high at Marko's funeral, for Christ's sake. Everyone saw you. They saw me holding you up. How can I marry you?"

"Who said I want to marry you?" Tatiana's voice was more distant and slurred from the beating and the growing effects of whatever she injected. "At that funeral, I had to get high. I am so sick of listening to the jokes behind my back. They all say them just loud enough for me to hear. All those wives and fucking mistresses laughing at me. They all think you're a fag, you know. You spend all that time at the strip club, and you fuck no one. Imagine if they found out that you don't even touch me. Imagine if they found out you can't even touch me with the help of that Viagra. Maybe you are gay, and I am what they call a beard."

"Shut up, you filthy junkie. Shut up!"

"Homo. Queer. Cocksuc—"

There was a sudden gurgling and then the sound of Igor screaming. Water sloshed inside, and a mist sprayed through the screen on the kitchen window. Igor was drowning Tatiana in the sink. After half a minute, I heard a gasp and a wet cough.

"You watch your mouth. Just watch what you say. I want you clean when I get home. Clean and with dinner in the oven. You know what that is, right? It's where I'll put your head next time you talk to me that way."

There was more coughing and the sound of the front door slamming. I hurried around the side of the house and saw the yellow car reverse onto the road before rocketing out towards the core.

I ran across the street and got in the Volvo. Within a minute, I was at a light, three cars behind the yellow BMW. I was used to Igor's erratic driving, and I let him get ahead knowing I would catch up at the next light. No amount of speed would get anyone through all greens downtown — the timing wasn't there. As I drove, I thought about Igor. Tatiana let slip the fact that he was impotent. That jived with everything Igor had said in the hospital room and everything I had noticed about him. His life was all one big masculine front. The yellow sports car, the aggressive driving, the strip club office he had. Everything was an attempt to convey a message of masculinity. Tatiana said wives and mistresses thought he was gay; that meant Igor's facade wasn't fooling anyone. But he wasn't gay; he wasn't always like he was, he was mind-fucked from being shot in the shoulder and left to die. Being in a gunfight and losing had hurt something inside him, something he believed he needed to kill me in order to get back.

I had met men like Igor before: pros who lost control of a situation and could no longer cope with the job. Soldiers and cops called it post-traumatic stress disorder. Problem was, our job didn't have benefits or a retirement plan, and none of us had a shot at a real job and an ordinary life. Most of the people like Igor either went down on the job, or they did it to themselves. They didn't even need to pull the trigger most times. They just showed the wrong people that they couldn't be trusted, and it would get done for them. No pro was going to let some cracked egg take them down. If they already knew too much about a job, it just made sense to kill them before they compromised the workers or the paycheque. There were no retirement parties or gold watches, just a loud send-off moving at a few hundred metres per second.

Igor went another way. He got some kind of insight into himself and learned about closure. He figured killing me would reboot him. Missing a second chance at murdering me must have pushed him even closer to the edge.

Igor's mental state aside, it was clear that he was an earner. The bags coming into the strip club were numerous. Enough for Sergei Vidal to keep a squirrely maniac on the payroll. Money trumps crazy every time.

For a few seconds I was a car length behind Igor and saw a phone to his ear. He was still on it when he parked behind the Steel City Lounge. I waited on the side of the road, watching through the chain link fence for him to get off the phone. Seventeen minutes later, Igor hung up and walked to the club. I reversed up the street and found a spot on a side road near where I had parked the day before. I caught up to Igor and joined the ranks of a rowdy softball team, ten feet behind him, who had decided to celebrate a win with beers and g-strings. Igor glanced our way, but he never made me. I was invisible within arm's reach.

I spent seven hours inside the Steel City Lounge. More bags came in, and even more flesh jiggled by. Igor never looked my way, and no one bothered me in my spot. Igor left late and alone again, and his crew left a bit after him carrying nothing.

I didn't follow anyone home. Instead, I drove out towards the Flamboro Downs Racetrack. A few years back, an unlicensed veterinarian patched my arm up after I got tagged by a bullet. She was a down-on-her-luck drunk, and she would do almost anything for money.

The drive took just under an hour. I pulled into her driveway at 3:30 a.m. and pounded on the front door. The knocking woke up several neighbourhood farm dogs, and I heard horses from the barn neigh and snort. I pounded again, thinking I had to rouse Maggie from a drunken sleep. What happened next I wasn't prepared for. A man opened the door.

"Who the fuck are you?"

"I need to see Maggie," I said. I said it with confidence, like I had an appointment. Most people will overlook almost anything if it seems official, even being woken out of bed at three in the morning. This guy wasn't one of those people.

"That's not what I asked you. I asked who you were."

"I have business with Maggie." I stopped trying to sound confident and turned my shoulders. My right hand hung near the .45 holster. There was a chance that Maggie could be patching someone else's bullet wounds. I looked the man up and down and checked the blackness behind him for any movement. The man was shirtless, soft, and wearing only Toronto Maple Leaf boxer shorts. Both of his hands were empty and visible, and he had an erection. I had woken the guy up, and he was no pro. Anyone getting a bullet patched by Maggie would make her open the door while they stood inside with a gun on her. They would get her to send me away. They wouldn't open the door with only their boner pointing at me.

"Charlie?" a woman's voice said from inside, breaking the tension.

"You get back to the bedroom. I'm dealing with this."

"But, Charlie, who is it?"

"You do what I tell you. I have this."

"I need to see Maggie," I said.

"Me?" I heard her say.

"Damn it! I'm calling the police."

Maggie appeared over the man's shoulder, and I could see things were different. As her eyes widened and remembered me, I saw the lack of broken blood vessels in her face, her healthy hair, and her thinner body. She had cleaned herself up. I ground my teeth realizing she wasn't what I needed her to be anymore.

"Charlie, this is just an old client. He probably needs something for his horse. You put that phone down and go back to bed. I'll be back inside in a sec."

"Banging on the door at this hour, he's lucky I didn't shoot him."

"I know, baby. Go back to bed." She walked outside in her bathrobe and closed the door. "What do you want?" Her tone was cold and flat.

"You look good. Being clean agrees with you," I said.

"What do you want? I don't do what you need anymore."

"Doesn't change a thing," I said.

"It changes everything."

"No, it doesn't. What you did is what you do. That kind of work never goes away. You'll still do it, just maybe not for money." I opened my coat, and she saw the .45.

"Oh, my God."

"He's not here. It's just you, me, and Charlie."

"Charlie," she whispered.

"I need one thing, and I'm gone," I said. "This time I'll stay gone. I understand you've changed, I accept that. But I'm here now, and that is something you have to accept."

"Charlie doesn't know what I did. The things I done."

"Get me what I need and he won't learn it from me."

She sighed, and her shoulders sagged. "What do you want?"

"Ketamine and a syringe," I said.

"You on the stuff? That shit ain't for fooling around with. It's dangerous."

"I need it and I'm gone."

"I don't feel right about this. I'm no drug dealer."

"You were a lot of things. I just need you to be one thing for a few minutes more."

She looked at the house, then at me. "Come on out to the barn," she said.

Maggie threw on some shoes from behind the door, led me out to the barn and into a room filled with stainless steel. She opened a cabinet and gave me a vial along with a syringe in a sterilized paper packet.

"Here, now I'm a drug dealer." She started to cry.

"If I were to inject an animal, where would be the best place to bury the needle?"

"What? An animal?"

"A two-hundred-pound animal that needs to be out cold fast."

I couldn't fool her. "Oh, no. You can't. It's too dangerous. You could kill a person."

"Without this, that will be the only option."

She thought about it. "A quarter of the bottle will put a man down if you get him in the neck."

"How fast?"

"Twenty seconds. He'll be limp, and he'll hallucinate terribly while he's under. Too much and you'll put him in a coma . . . or worse."

I put the vial and syringe in my pocket. "You look good. I hope it's permanent," I said. "I promise I won't be back."

I left to the sound of Maggie sobbing. I was back at the motel by 4:30 and back at Igor's by 9 a.m.

CHAPTER **TEN**

I t was eight at night when Igor jogged out to his banana
BMW and screeched away from the house. I followed
behind, catching up at the lights. Igor was on his phone
again, and from the nodding and shaking of his head, I
could see that it was an animated conversation.

He parked on a side street and walked into the Steel
City Lounge by 8:15. I gave him room and waited until
9:00 to go inside. The street clothes I had changed into
made me just another guy looking to blow off steam after
work. When I took my seat, I saw that it would be different tonight. The VIP lounge was roped off, but there were
no girls upstairs. Two men stood on guard behind the
velvet rope, smoking and scanning the crowd. Every
twenty minutes, a man appeared from behind them, said a
few words, nodded, then retreated back where he came
from. There was a room upstairs, and something important was happening inside. Forty-five minutes later, Igor
appeared on the balcony towing a large duffel bag. The
bag was much bigger than any that had come in during the

last few days. Judging by the way Igor rubbed his shoulder when he set it down, it was heavy.

I didn't get up until Igor started lugging the bag down the stairs. I threw down a ten to cover the drink and walked outside. I ran to the Volvo, drove fast around front, and found a spot on the street in front of the strip club where I could watch for Igor. I loaded the syringe while I sat waiting in the car. If he had more than one bodyguard come along with the money, I wouldn't be able to use the ketamine. What I had planned would only work if Igor had no alibi. I had seen grifters do part of it time and time again. The set-up played on human nature and the social instincts grilled into Canadians since birth. The rest would play out on its own.

I swore under my breath when Igor came out flanked by the two men who stood watch upstairs in the VIP lounge. Igor held the bag himself, over his shoulder, and marched under the bulk of the cash in the duffel. I started the car, leaving the lights off, and checked the mirrors. Two guards was bad — it meant there would have to be a change in plans.

I crept up the street behind the three men and let them turn down Mary Street towards the parking lot and Igor's car. The Volvo nosed around the corner, and I saw Igor shoving the bag into the passenger seat of his car. The BMW was cramped when it was just Igor and Tatiana; there was no way the money would ride shotgun while the two men rode in back. Igor slid in after the money and started the car. The bodyguards stayed on the street, and one of them slapped the roof twice. They each took two steps back from the car to give it room to back up. I stopped thinking about how to deal with the bodyguards and quickly accelerated past the men in the street. Igor was taking the money alone to Sergei. It made sense given what I knew about Igor. He tried to prove to the world that he was a man twenty-four seven. That kind of guy would bring the money alone because he would want everyone to see what a success he was. Having bodyguards come too might spread out the accolades. No matter how stupid carrying that much cash alone was, his ego wouldn't let him be rational.

I used two side roads to get on Barton Street ahead of Igor and waited in the jail parking lot to see which way he would go. Thirty seconds went by before Igor pulled around the corner towards me. I put the parking brake on, got out, and began crossing the street. The needle was out in my fist along the side of my leg; my thumb was on the plunger. The yellow BMW tore up the street, and I picked up the pace. It might have been the lack of sleep that made walking into the path of Igor's car so easy; it might just as easily have been the adrenaline high from being on the grind again instead of just rebounding. My face pulled into a familiar grin as I stumbled in front of the car and bent my knees, ready to dive if Igor didn't slow down. Igor saw me in the path of the headlights and hit the brakes. I jumped in the air and let the rapidly slowing car catch me with its hood. My body rolled up to the windshield and raced back down to the pavement.

The door opened, and Igor was out. "What the fuck? Are you crazy? How did you not see me? If you dented the car, I'm going to kill you."

Igor played into the second typical response. When grifters faked being hit, they hoped for the usual Canadian response: a mortified, polite, apologetic driver. Even if it wasn't their fault, most Canadians will think it was and offer to help the victim — even though the real victim is them. Nine times out of ten, drivers will cut cheques to get away without involving the cops. The money keeps them safe from the law and their conscience. But the other type of driver was Igor's type. They could care less about other people. They only cared about themselves and their cars. I didn't care which response I got out of Igor; it wasn't a grift, I didn't want money — I wanted him.

While Igor checked the car over, I clawed at his pants and pulled myself to my knees. I wasn't hurt, but Igor didn't know that. He turned towards me and got even more irate. "Get the fuck off me!" Igor tried to shove me back, but I surged off my knees, coming up under his right arm. My left hand came around his back and took a fistful of his hair while my right hand slammed the syringe into the side of his neck. I forced Igor against the hood as I pushed the plunger down with my thumb and sent half the bottle of ketamine into the Russian's neck. I expected Maggie to recommend the smallest dose possible in an effort to ease her conscience, so I doubled her prescription, figuring half the vial would be enough to do the job but probably not enough to kill him.

When my thumb wouldn't go any further into the syringe, I let go of the needle and wrapped my arm around Igor, pinning his left arm to his body. Igor thrashed and bucked, but the hood of the car held him upright, and my body, pressed against his, gave him no room to move. He was strong at first, but he began to weaken after a few seconds. Within ten seconds, he was drooping in my arms. I dragged him to the passenger side, shoved him in the car, on top of the duffel, and got in behind him. I drove the car off the street into the jail parking lot, watching distant onlookers stare at the car from the rear-view mirror until the wheels hit the jail parking lot. Contact with the jail sent many of the people on their way, as though what had happened had made some sort of sense. A few other stragglers still stared at the parking lot and fished in their pockets for phones. I turned the BMW off and put the keys in Igor's pocket. I got out of the car and reached in for a handful of Igor's hair and shirt. My hands pulled him into the driver's seat and buckled him in. Then I pulled the bag across his lap and onto the pavement. Igor's chest was rising and falling, and his pulse was still easy to find. He whimpered in the chemical daze while I pulled the syringe from his neck and closed the door. The drugs, working their way deeper into Igor's system, turned his muscles to jelly and sent the Russian forward until his head hit the steering wheel.

The duffel was heavy as I carried it to the Volvo. I put it in the passenger seat, disengaged the parking brake, and drove out of the lot, using the second exit, towards the motel. The whole grab took under three minutes. I figured some of the witnesses might call the cops, but there would be nothing left for them but a drunk sleeping it off in his car.

On the way to the motel, I powered up the cell phone and dialled Detective Sergeant Morrison's cell number. "Morrison?"

He picked up on the second ring.

"You find anything on that name I gave you?"

"Igor? There's a few Igors, but I know the one you asked about. Seems to be in charge of drug revenue. He's not dumb though, I can't find a house in his name or any employment records. All I could find out was that he was a fill-in for some mope that got shot in a Russian bar, and since then he's been holding his own."

"Who told you this?"

"Couple a cops. And a few CI's."

"Who's the cop?"

"Fuck you."

"Miller?" I asked. No response came. "How about the

CI's? Are they in the mix or just people with ears?"

"They're in the mix enough to be at that funeral you crashed. We ain't finished, you know."

I ignored him. "Did you play up that kidnapping angle that we talked about?"

Morrison sighed. "Yeah."

"So the cops think whoever took me killed the nurse too?"

"Until I can prove different. And I can prove different whenever I want. You know that, right?"

I pressed on. "Why did they take me?"

"We figure you saw too much. So did the nurse. See? What I say goes."

"Who's running the investigation?"

"I am."

"So we're almost done."

"I told you we ain't finished, not by a fucking long shot, mate."

I ignored him again. "How fast can you get in touch with your CI's?"

"Why?" Morrison dropped the base and anger from his voice. He sensed the promise of a bust.

"Spread the word that Igor took some money that didn't belong to him."

"What money? How much? Where'd it come from?" The questions came hard and fast.

"Just put the word out tonight. You have four hours to do it."

"Why four hours? If you know something about Igor, tell me."

"Morrison, do one other thing."

"Tell me what you know."

"Let slip to Miller that Igor is on the outs and you heard Sergei Vidal is after him personally."

MIKE KNOWLES

Morrison's anger flared. "You keep trying to put every-thing on Miller like I'm supposed to believe you over him. He's been with me every step of the way. He's saved my life more than once, and his kids call me uncle. I told you before, Miller is a good cop."

"Then you got nothing to worry about. Just let it slip casually later on tonight. If you do this, you'll get your fish."

"When? Who's the fucking fish?"

I hung up the phone and drove the rest of the way to the motel. Morrison trusted the fat cop. It was more than just the brotherhood of blue banding together against a crook like me, they had history on and off the job. He had blinders on about the idea of Miller double dipping. I just hoped that Morrison's need for a big bust would push him past his myopia enough to leak what I told him to say to Miller. He broke a lot of rules, and put himself on the line, to get me to work with him, so I figured he'd use Miller too if there was no other way. Morrison was greedy, and he'd find a way to rationalize telling Miller what I said to get what he wanted. If he really felt Miller was clean, he would decide there would be no harm in telling him anything because it would go nowhere. But if Morrison did have any doubts about his partner, what I said would push them to the surface. Using Miller kept Morrison off balance and out of focus. I needed to keep pushing him so he stayed off his game.

Back at the motel, I pulled the duffel into the room. The bag was big enough to take up most of the space in front of the tiny bed. I closed the blinds and unzipped the bag. Inside were packets of cash, all denominations sepa-rated by bill and bound with paper bands. Igor had been on his way to a big drop. One thing was for sure, the money would be missed.

There was nothing else in the bag with the money. I

checked the pockets and the liner to be sure. I had been burned by a hidden GPS in a bag before, and it wouldn't happen again. Satisfied there was no GPS, I put all of the cash back in the bag and zipped it up. This money was going to be chum in the water. This much couldn't go missing without repercussions, and Igor would be on the hook for it alone because he left with it in his tiny yellow sports car. There was no way he could pay it back either — it was too much cash for Igor just to take out of a bank account and replace. The missing money would do two things: it would put Igor at odds with his boss, and it would force him to do something stupid. Igor was an emotional wreck; I figured a failure of this magnitude would push him over the edge. He would have to do something crazy to stay alive, and I was going to be there when he went for it. I needed something big to shake Morrison off me, and Igor would get it for me. I had to use whatever scheme Igor came up with to take him out of the game, because eventually he would pass off blame on me for the money being gone. If Sergei Vidal believed him, it would be a short jump for the synapses in his brain to connect me to the robbery years ago that reignited war between the Russians and the Italians. Then I would be up against the whole Russian mob instead of just one sick head case.

The radio alarm clock bolted to the bedside table told me I had just over three hours until Igor's vitamin K–induced sleep should start to wear off. I put the money in the trunk and drove to the closest drug store. Inside, I bought caffeine pills and Red Bull. I stood in the parking lot chewing the pills and washing them down with swigs of the cola. I had been on too many stakeouts for too many days, and the shitty food and shittier bed were catching up with me. I had to wrap this up soon, or I would slip up.

116

When my hands began to open and close on their own, I got behind the wheel and rode the caffeine buzz all the way to the Barton Street Jail.

On my first pass, I saw the yellow BMW parked where I left it. It was 11:35 p.m., and traffic on the street was minimal. I slipped into a space across the street and watched the car — nothing moved for six hours. The extra large dose of ketamine did its job better than I expected. Just before six in the morning, the door opened, and Igor fell into the street. He threw up and then pulled himself up off the ground using a tire and the hood for help. When he was vertical, he massaged the side of his neck in between dry heaves. After one particularly nasty bout of vomiting, his head snapped towards the car, and he stumbled to the open door. He looked inside, through the driver seat, to the passenger side, then into the cramped back seats, and finally into the trunk. From inside the Volvo I heard the scream that followed. Igor pulled out his cell phone and thumbed it frantically. He never moved his lips. Instead, he put the phone to his ear and just listened. After thirty seconds, he collapsed against the side of the car as though the phone had just dealt him a nasty physical blow. Someone on the other end of that phone was looking for Igor; worse, they were looking for the money.

CHAPTER ELEVEN

I sat up straighter and got ready to see how the Russian would play this. Igor closed the phone and stumbled behind the wheel. He could go one of two ways: back home, or towards whoever it was he was going to see before I robbed him. The yellow BMW trickled out of the parking lot towards Igor's house.

I let the BMW stay six car lengths ahead of me and watched as it swerved in and out of lanes. Igor usually cut in and out of traffic with razor-sharp precision, but the BMW was not making those expert merges anymore. The car was making lane changes that started too far back and involved Igor riding the medians between two lanes for too long before he finally tugged the wheel enough to get into the next lane. The drugs were still heavily in his system, and they had screwed with Igor's perception and reaction time; they didn't affect his lead foot. Igor ran two red lights and made it home a full minute before I caught up. I left the car behind the ice cream shack and circled around the back of the house to the kitchen window.

I kept low until I was underneath the sill. I stole glances inside, but I couldn't see Igor anywhere. I scanned the yard for any neighbours who would be able to see me from their breakfast table, but the trees covered me. I let my head slowly creep up towards the window so I could take a longer look inside when a window two stories above me shattered. Pieces of glass fell, along with flowers and water from what used to be a full vase, onto the lawn. I hustled to the side of the house and around to the front door while Igor's screams poured out of the now jaggedly open window.

I climbed onto the side of the porch, accessible from the corner of the house, and walked towards the front door, head low, as though I belonged there. The unlocked doorknob noiselessly turned under my palm, and as soon as my body cleared the door, I had the Colt out. The big pistol followed my eyes through the first floor — finding nothing. All the while, I could hear Igor yelling upstairs. I took a spot beside the staircase, impossible to see from upstairs, and listened.

"On the take? On the take! Why would I be on the take? Who is saying such things?"

There was a pause while Igor heard a response in his ear.

"How is it all over the streets?"

Another pause.

"Well, how does some fuck at that shitty bar know anything?"

Pause.

"Where else? At the Strip Club! Holy shit!" Igor's curse was breathless as though the words left his mouth with every bit of air in his lungs. "We have to stop this before it gets to Sergei."

Pause.

"What did he ask you?" Igor was starting to squeal. "Well, what did you tell him?"

MIKE KNOWLES

Pause.

"What do you mean you said you didn't know where I was?"

Pause.

"I don't care if it was Pietro who was asking. You work for me, no one else! If anyone asks about me, you say I had business to handle, but it is finished tonight. You hear that? Tonight. Everything is back to normal tonight. Put that out to everyone and shut up whoever is doing the talking."

There was a long pause.

"What do you mean there was a cop looking for me too? What cop? Was he a fat pig of a man?"

Pause.

"So who was he? Does anyone know him?"

Pause.

"Who talked to him?"

Pause.

"Did Pietro see the cop?"

There was one last silence before I heard Igor scream "Fuck" so loud that I knew it meant the call was over.

Christ, Morrison was a mover. I had leaked a single first name two days ago, and he was already catching up to me. I saw that his playing loose with the rules in the hospital was, in his mind, a safe bet because he was a born hunter of men, able to turn a name into an address almost overnight. He never had a doubt in his mind that he wouldn't be able to track me down the same way he found Igor. But I wasn't like Igor. He was a mid-level collector with an organization holding him up and watching his back. I was a different breed, a grinder. I survived for decades without a safety net to keep me from falling to my death. I was bred to survive in the dark, and there was no cop who would round me up in a day. But if Morrison proved any more capable than I thought him to be, he would find himself being chased with a worse sentence than jail time not far behind. Morrison wasn't just my problem anymore. Igor had to share the load, but the Russian also had to deal with Pietro. He was one of Sergei Vidal's bodyguards that I saw stored in the memory of the cop's camera. His presence meant a noose was forming around Igor's neck.

"What's wrong, baby? Bad night?" From my spot below, I could hear that Tatiana's accented voice was slow and slurred — she was still high from the night before.

"Shut up, junkie."

"You're the one who's yelling. I'm just trying to open the lines of communication like Doctor Davis said."

"Shut up."

"You strike out at that lame-ass strip club of yours? One of the girls find out that you are dickless? Is that it?" The doctor's lessons were apparently over. Tatiana laughed with the humour and courage that only a needle could supply.

"Everything is falling apart, baby." Igor sounded on the verge of tears.

"Ha. Are you crying, you little bitch? That is such a turnoff, you know? Aw, does Baby Igor need his baby bottle?" Tatiana broke into a case of the giggles that only stopped when Igor spoke again, sounding sad and pathetic.

"Seriously, I need you."

Tatiana did a slurred impression of Igor. "Seriously, I need you." She tried to laugh at him again, but only a gurgle came from her throat.

"Stupid, fucking whore!"

Tatiana's body rolled down the stairs without warning. She landed with her eyes shut. They stayed closed as I backed away into the kitchen. Igor thumped down the stairs and dragged Tatiana's unconscious body into the kitchen. I stood down the hallway, in the mudroom off the garage, watching the carnage.

"I come to you with my needs. I try to be open. I try to communicate. I do everything Dr. Davis said to do, and you laugh at me. Me! Let's see you laugh at this."

Igor turned on the gas burner and shoved Tatiana face first towards the hot element.

"I'll show you how to cook with the stove since all you know how to do is heat up that junk you shove in your arm."

Tatiana screamed and came out of her semi-conscious state. She bounced off the burner and came back at Igor like a feral cat. Her hands clawed at his face, and she screamed guttural obscenities at him. Igor screamed as her nails found his cheeks. He flailed at the girl, then shoved her back into the stove again. Tatiana showed she was as hard as the Soviet hammer on the old flag. She picked up a kettle off the stove top and swung it like a haymaker into the side of Igor's head. The impact of the stainless steel appliance opened the Russian's stitches and sent water onto the floor along with Igor's ass. He turned onto his stomach and tried to get up while Tatiana kicked him.

"No more! No more! I am tired of you whining because the whole world knows you are a pussy. And when you can't get anything done, you realize the world is right, so you come home and beat me. Well, no more. How do you like getting hit, you pussy? You faggot! You motherfucker!"

Igor covered up and staggered to his feet. He silenced Tatiana with a backhand — putting her down hard. He tried to kick her, but he slipped on the water from the kettle and went down beside her.

Tatiana was still yelling. "How many times did I have to make you pull the trigger? How many times did I have to hold your hand so you could do your job? You are not a man. You could not even kill a man chained to a hospital bed. If it weren't for me the police would have found you crying in those handcuffs. You are a fool, a coward, and I hate you."

"Shut up!" Igor screamed. He took two handfuls of Tatiana's hair and used her head to steady himself getting up. She screamed as her head took all of his weight. Igor spread his feet wide and pulled Tatiana up to the stove. He again put her face down on the burner. She screamed and bucked, but Igor never let her go.

"Say something now! Say something! I didn't need you for anything, you junkie whore."

Smoke came up from the burner, and the smell of burnt hair and flesh wafted down the hall. Igor kept holding the girl down even though she had gone into shock and stopped struggling. I didn't move from my spot in the mudroom. Tatiana said it herself; she had to push Igor to pull the trigger. She had to hold his hand. She helped create a monster, and now her creation was returning the favour. She was as ugly as Igor, and, like the rest of us, she deserved worse than she got.

Igor finally let the girl go, and she fell soundlessly to the floor. He picked up the kettle she hit him with and held it over his head with two hands. He let out a scream as he crashed down on Tatiana and beat her to death.

CHAPTER TWELVE

had Igor cold. He had just murdered an accomplice to countless crimes in the middle of his kitchen. But how easily could Morrison connect Igor to the mob? He said himself that he had little on Igor. There were rumours about his being a drug dealer for the Russians, but no real paper trail existed. Igor wasn't going to be enough for Morrison, not like this. I needed more.

All I had to go on was the missing money. The money would lead me to someone bigger than Igor. When they dealt with him, I would have something to trade Morrison that would connect all of the pieces.

Igor sobbed, bent over the counter. He went on like that for five minutes. When he was finished, he dried his eyes on his sleeve and looked at Tatiana. "Stupid junkie," he said. "Look where your mouth got you."

He walked away from the body, sat at the kitchen table, dialled a number into his cell phone, and waited.

"I need to see you," he said after a minute. "I don't care if it's early, I need to see you."

Pause.

"No, you listen, pig. You're on my payroll. That means you work for me. Now get your fat ass out of bed and get over to my house. We have things to discuss."

Igor hung up the phone and walked away from the table. While he was in sight, I watched him peer over the counter at the body of Tatiana. He shook his head and then went up the stairs. A few minutes later, I heard the sound of running water. I stayed downstairs with Tatiana while Igor showered and cleaned up. I stayed out of the blood and the mess as I worked my way through each drawer in the kitchen. In the back of the drawer beside the fridge, I found instruction manuals and warranties for all of the major appliances. Underneath the manuals in their ripped plastic sheaths, I found a book. The spine was creased, and the pages were dog-eared and heavily high-lighted. Igor had worn out his copy of *I'm Okay, You're Okay*. I read the back cover and realized that Igor believed that he had adopted a "position" about himself that deter-mined how he felt about everything. His position was listed as "I'm not okay — you're okay." This kind of posi-tion was said, by the back of the book, to contaminate rational capabilities and leave people open to inappropri-ate emotional reactions. I wondered if trying to kill me in the hospital or killing a girlfriend was something Igor con-sidered to be an inappropriate emotional reaction. The book must have been the gateway to the doctor Tatiana was screaming about. For me, the book was just another window into Igor's broken mind. I wiped the book with my sleeve, put it back, and went on to the next drawer. Inside, I found a spare set of house keys with the second set of dealer keys for the BMW. I pocketed both, went through the rest of the drawers, and got back to the mud-room before Igor came downstairs. He walked right

126

through the mess to make himself breakfast. He was eating toast when there was a knock at the door. I heard Igor get up to open it. Someone was let in, and two men stood in the foyer talking.

"I don't like meeting you like this — it's dangerous."

"Shut up."

"Seriously, I'm not just talking about cops. Word is Sergei is looking for you."

"Where did you hear that?" Igor sounded panicked.

"Cops at the station heard it on the street. What the hell did you do?"

"There was a complication."

"Did that complication scratch up your face like that?"

"No, that was Tatiana."

"Hunh, I always knew that bitch liked it kinky."

"Not anymore."

Igor walked back into the kitchen, sat, and pulled his chair up to the table. There was a long pause while Igor's guest looked at the body. I moved my head out just enough to see what I already knew was there. The man had his ample back to me as he looked in front of the stove. The huge mass of cop was covered in the same worn shitty suit I had seen when I first opened my eyes in the hospital. Detective Miller was Igor's rat in the department.

"What the fuck happened? Did you do this?"

"She did it to herself."

"I can't be a part of this. You fucking murder a chick, your chick, in your kitchen, then call me over. I'll go down as an accessory."

"You can go down as a crooked cop too. I have tapes and witnesses of you taking my money and getting me around police search and seizures. So you can maybe go down for her, or you can for sure go down because of me."

"Shit. Shit!" Miller said.

"We're both in the shit, but we can get out. I just need cash."

"How much?"

"A lot. I need a load of cash to pay Sergei for the loss and the embarrassment. It's money I do not have."

"So we're fucked."

"No, detective, I just need to know where there is a lot of money so that I can take it."

"You want me to help you steal money?"

"No wonder you are a detective. You are very smart. I wonder if you are smart enough to tell me who it was that was looking for me in my club tonight."

"How the fuck would I know?"

"It was a cop."

"Shit, it must have been Morrison. He came to me the other day and asked me about you. Well, he asked about a man named Igor; he didn't know any specifics, but I figured he meant you."

"And what did you tell him?"

"Nothing. I told him there were a lot of Igors. It's fucking true enough, your mothers weren't that creative back home. I said I'd look into it and get back to him."

"Why is he after me?" Igor asked.

"He wouldn't say."

"So how did he find me then?"

"Fucking guy is a police beast. He finds whatever he's looking for. What's fucked up is why he didn't talk to me about his lead on the strip club."

"Maybe you are not trusted," Igor said.

"Fuck that, Igor. Me and Morrison are tight. He eats at my house twice a week, for Christ's sake."

"Does he know about our deals?"

"Hell no!"

"Then you are not all that tight, *da*?"

MIKE KNOWLES

"Don't give me that Russian shit. That accent doesn't fool me. You grew up here, Igor. You're about as Russian as that red fucking salad dressing. Let me deal with Morrison. I'll get him off your back while you get the money," Miller said.

"Where will I be getting my money?"

"If you need it fast, then we got to hit the chinks."

"I'm listening."

"I got word the other day that the Fat Cobra Society are moving a lot of product out of the Secret Garden downtown."

I knew the gang. The Fat Cobra Society had branched out from San Francisco in the seventies. It found Canadian homes in Vancouver and Toronto, and its tentacles had gripped Hamilton sometime in the last decade. The Fat Cobra Society wasn't a punk street gang. It was organized and hostile. It ran women, drugs, and black market goods to the Asian community, and business was good. Hamilton was home to a large Asian population, especially after Columbia University opened its doors in West Hamilton. Columbia University was a boarding school for immigrant kids from all over the world who needed time to acclimatize to Canada before attending nearby McMaster University. Most of the students were Asian, and most of them got their illegal shit from someone with a familiar face.

"The police are watching the place?"

"No, I just found out from a CI. No one knows but me."

"Why haven't you told anyone?"

"I wanted to see how I could spin it. I like Chinese food, Chinese women, I figure I'll like their money too. But money's worth as much as rice if my ass is in jail. Word is the place is full of cash — full of it. Product and guns too. So you and your guys hit the Secret Garden tonight, take the slants by surprise, and you get your payday. With your crew, there will be enough manpower to get the job done fast and quiet."

"No crew, just us."

"Us? Fuck us. I can't have no part in this. This is your problem, your show. Why can't you use your guys?"

"If Sergei is after me, as you say, then they will be after me as well. They will be looking to kill me so that they can have my spot. It is common practice."

"I can't rob the triads outright. They'll kill me, if I don't get arrested first."

"I will do the robbing; you will just help me get inside by thinning the ranks. Don't worry, all will appear legal."

The two men spent an hour hashing out a plan to hit the Secret Garden. If they cared about the dead body lying in front of the stove, it never came up. I waited, listening, until Miller left and Igor went back upstairs. I slipped out back and got to the Volvo unseen. I left Igor at his house and drove back to the motel. On the way I thought about what Miller had said. Morrison left him in the dark about the reasons behind his search for Igor. That meant whatever bond they had was being stretched. He still hadn't found Igor, so he had no way of knowing how corrupt Miller was, but a few more days of off-the-clock hunting would be enough time for him to find Igor's house. Luckily for me, Igor didn't have a few days. I got back to the motel and dove straight onto the lumpy bed. I needed sleep if I was going to be having Chinese for dinner.

MIKE KNOWLES

slept for four hours, put on my clothes, and went for a late lunch at the Secret Garden. It was a hole-in-the-wall place on Main Street, just down from a few really good Chinese food restaurants. I walked the streets and noticed the same three faces outside the restaurant each time I was nearby. They never noticed me because on each pass I was farther and farther away. The first pass was in front of the building. The second, ten minutes later, was from across the street. The third pass was done in a cab. We rode by twice, the first time watching the men I saw, the second eyeing the area for what I would need.

The three Chinese men were in their forties with tall bushy hair and tight leather motorcycle jackets. Two of the men stood near the entrance of the restaurant — one in front of the door, the other fifteen metres away in the mouth of an alley. Both had black hair that they had let grow long in the back. They accentuated the mullet with wisps of hair combed over one of their eyes. The men were similar in height, weight, and style. The only difference was the tattoo that showed on the neck of the man in front of the alley. The third guard was on the opposite side of the building. His hair was bleached and sculpted high on his head. The hair was very white, and I saw no roots, meaning the job had been done recently. The heavy leather made it impossible to tell if the men were carrying — I figured it was a safe bet that they were.

"Never guess anything that will make your life easier. The world has a way of making sure things stay as shitty as possible, remember that." My uncle's voice was still as loud now as it was when he was alive.

The three men were a constant; customers were not. On every pass, I never saw anyone getting any food from the Secret Garden. There was an old woman behind the counter wearing an apron, but it was white — too white to belong to a cook. Miller's intel had been good. He knew about the three men out front, making me think what he had said about inside was probably true too.

On my fifth pass, again on foot, I walked inside the Secret Dragon. The old woman behind the counter looked at me, then into the back, then at me again.

"I help you?"

"An order of rice and sweet and sour chicken."

"We no have sweet and sour chicken."

"Just the rice then."

"No rice."

I blew out a bit of air and put my smile on. "Okay, just get me a plate of whatever you have."

"Food cost a lot of money."

"That's cool."

"Food take a lot of time."

"I'll wait."

The woman disappeared into the back and was gone for five minutes. I used the time, and the small spaces between the lettering on the window, to look out at the men out front. They were tense because of my arrival, but they never left their posts; they stayed on duty outside the restaurant. The woman came back with a small Styrofoam container that cost ten dollars. The container was cold to the touch, and when I opened it across the street, and around the corner, I saw that it was some kind of meat in brown sauce. They had added a live cockroach for flavour too. I chuckled at the move and left the container open on the concrete. Birds descended on the open container, eager for a free meal. They got close enough to the container to see what it was, then left it alone.

The front served expensive, shitty food with service that paralleled the worst orphanage cafeteria line. People got the message to stay away in rude stereo. Miller had explained that the men out front were the primary security force. The men inside were mostly money counters. There were only three other armed guards behind the counter. The men outside watched who came in and out; if you tried a stick-up, they would be behind you waiting in the streets. If you took a run at any of the three men out front first, the money would be run out back by one of the armed guards, and the other two gunmen would back up the men in the street. The Secret Garden was a good front with satisfactory protection and not a lot of overhead. The main deterrent was not the men but the triad's reputation.

Igor was going to take money from a well-sourced, dangerous group of people, and he had to do it without help too. His own crew would be as dangerous to him as the Fat Cobra Society, but worse than that, if someone figured out that Igor worked for Sergei, pride would dictate a gang war. Then it wouldn't matter if Igor got the money back. Sergei would kill him ten times over for stirring up the Asian hornet nest.

I waited around the corner for just the right kind of truck. There weren't many big stores downtown that operated outside Jackson Square Mall. Most of the shops were mom-and-pop run, and they got stock in via the family minivan every week or so. I had to wait the better part of an hour for a U-Haul, the largest the company supplied, to lumber down the street. Traffic was slower than usual because of the people driving back home to their apartments in the core or driving through to their nicer homes on the fringes of the city. I let the U-Haul pass me and jogged into the temporary cover it provided as it rolled down the street. The angle of my body behind the U-Haul made seeing me impossible for the three men in front of the Secret Garden. The truck hit each pothole with a thunderous explosion of metal on worn out shocks. People ignored the sound and looked at something other than the orange and white truck with the large squid painted on the side that showed off the majesty of the aquatic life of Newfoundland. All of the U-Haul trucks had been painted recently. They each had images on the sides of the cabs that represented the different wild animals of Canada. The pictures were hideous, and they kept even more eyes off the truck in the same way a large facial mole forces people to look but not look.

Three storefronts up from the Secret Garden, I hooked, unseen by the guards, into a vacant storefront. The dark doorway was sunk two metres in, and the glass door still advertised a foreclosed decorative bead store called Bead Craft and Beyond. The smaller print underneath told me that the store was once the city's jewellery and decoration headquarters. The previous owner left notices up in the window about how-to beading classes and custom work that could be done to clothing. The store was like most others in the city — alive for a minute, then gone. The

MIKE KNOWLES

storefront would flicker with life a few more times over the next couple of years, I expected, until it finally became something more palatable to the city. When the vacancy was replaced by a Tim Hortons or a dollar store, it would finally stay occupied longer than a couple of months.

The doorway went back enough to keep me out of sight while I waited for Igor to show up. On either side of me, display windows went out to the sidewalk. I was able to look through the panes of glass beside me to see the Secret Garden. Miller had told Igor that the money came every day around lunch. It was counted, bagged, and picked up by eight. There would be a lot of cash, according to Miller, because this was the only money-counting front the Fat Cobra Society had in the city. Igor planned to show up just before eight. That way, the money would be together and already set up to move.

I spent a few hours in the darkness until I saw Igor, duffel bag in hand, walk past the Secret Garden. The leather-clad security out front didn't look at him more than once as he passed. Igor, on the other hand, stared openly. He even stopped in front of the restaurant to look for the third guard, who was standing out of sight, on his own doorstep, just up the street. When Igor was done his shitty scope, he crossed the street and took a spot on a bench four storefronts away from where I stood. The vacant storefront was perfect camouflage — he never saw me. Igor pulled out his phone and dialled a number. He said a few words before closing the phone and putting it back into his pocket.

I watched Igor sit for ten minutes until a wave of red light stabbed into my hiding place. An unmarked police car rolled down the street behind a large SUV. The SUV pulled to the curb, and the cop car pulled in behind, right in front of the Secret Garden. A huge man rocked his way out of the driver's seat of the cop car. Sergeant Miller was doing a traffic stop downtown.

Igor waited for Miller to get to the window of the SUV before getting up off his bench and crossing the street towards the Secret Garden. The three men out front saw him cross with the bag and enter the restaurant, brushing the arm of the fat cop as he walked over the sidewalk. Each guard stayed where he was, staring at the police lights and the fat cop. I could see through the window of the Secret Garden enough to make out Igor holding a gun. The guard closest to the restaurant saw it too, because he pulled a phone from his pocket and spoke into it using a walkie-talkie function. I watched the other two guards use their phones in a similar fashion. A rapid discussion broke out in Chinese. I knew what was on their minds. To stop the robbery, they would have to pull guns and rush past a cop to get inside. The cop would try to stop them, and that would cause them to break one of the only rules criminals have — never shoot a cop. You break that rule, and the whole weight of the police force will roll over you. Cops hold the line between the shit and everybody else, but if you go and make it personal, you'll find out they play dirtier than anyone on the street. They'll fuck you and make sure you get charged for not saying thank you. Everyone knows this, and it froze the Chinese men out front.

Inside, Igor had pistol whipped the old woman in the clean apron. Miller stood outside, with his back to the restaurant, holding the SUV driver's ID. He was moving the licence back and forth as though he were trying to focus his eyes without his glasses. Miller's stall kept the men out front, but they weren't standing still. One was still on his phone as he slowly approached the other two men and the restaurant entrance. Miller saw the men coming and went so far as to put his back against the glass for support while he wrote the ticket.

Igor had worked fast. He had an arm around the woman's neck as he headed towards the back room, gun pointed forward. He was following the plan he and Miller had devised back at his house. Igor would use the woman as a human shield while he took the money. Once he had the money, he would force everyone out the back door. He would lock them outside and then bolt out the front while Miller covered him with his bullshit traffic stop. As I crossed the street, Igor got a shoe inside the back room. When my foot crossed the median, I put three bullets, in one second, into Miller's unmarked police car.

The heavy .45 spit the slugs 250 metres per second, and the bang chased after the lead, shrieking a warning to everyone around. The sound of metal repeatedly piercing metal was obscured by the gunshots from across the street. Everyone looked around for the source of the sounds except Miller and Igor. Miller dropped the ticket pad from his hands and took cover behind his car while Igor spun his human shield around to face the street. I put two more bullets into the unmarked car's tires before letting three more rounds chew holes into the Secret Garden's windows. Drivers ducked their heads below their dashboards and stomped on the gas. Cars crashed into one another, and traffic ground to a halt all around the restaurant. I used one car — its occupants screaming on the floor — to crouch behind as I reloaded. As I took cover I pulled a fresh magazine from my pocket. The spent clip slipped into my hand, and I slid its replacement home. I pushed the spent magazine into my pocket, racked the slide, and came out from behind the car. The four seconds I wasted reloading gave the leather-clad Chinese men time to cross the street towards me. A bullet starred the windshield of the car I was behind as I stood. Another bullet, from a second shooter close to the first, shattered a window across the street behind me. I went to one knee and took a two-handed grip. Another bullet whizzed over my head and found the hood of a nearby car.

The man in front of me was trying to pick me off without getting any closer. He was probably used to shooting at new-to-the-life kids or ambitious junkies taking a shot at a refund. He expected me to run away from the bullets and straight into one of his partners. He had no way of knowing that this wasn't my first rodeo. I came up fast, sighted the man, and pulled the trigger once, then twice. Two heavy slugs punched him off his feet. The first hit centre mass, the second impacted high in the chest near the collar bone. As he fell, a mist of blood and bone fragments stained a white car behind him.

I turned and moved along the car, looking for the other guard who had taken a shot at me. Through the rear windshield I saw the man with the neck tattoo approaching. He held his gun in two shaky hands as he wove through the petrified gridlock. Terrified heads lifted enough to see the man moving, gun in hand, and then disappeared back below the windows. The guard was staying low and waving his gun with stiff movements in front, behind, and under each car he approached. I watched him advance on a small hybrid and waited for him to check the space in front of the bumper when gunfire got my attention. Thinking it was the third guard, I ducked back behind the car, but the shots weren't at me — a firefight had broken out in the Secret Garden. Flashes could be seen from behind what was left of the starred and broken glass. Some of the shots came from an automatic, making me think that in the confusion Igor lost control of the situation and the men in back had enough time to get to a weapon. Within seconds of another burst of automatic

chatter, Igor came running out of the Secret Garden —
without his bag. His grey shirt was bloody, but he still
managed a speedy getaway down the street. The guard
near the hybrid saw Igor running away in his bloody shirt
and turned his stiff-armed stance away from my direction
towards Igor's back. I rose off my knee, aiming just above
the tattoo, and put a bullet into the side of his head before
he could pull the trigger. The top of the man's head came
off, his scalp parting like leaves of cabbage.

Igor ignored the shot and kept on running. He turned
down the first side street he saw and vanished from sight.
I turned back to the store front and saw Miller on his feet,
police pistol in hand. His feet were spread wide, and one
eye was closed. I dove left as the muzzle flash erupted.
Behind the car, I felt my chest for any wet spots, but I
found none. I shuffled back and tried the door handle to
the car I used for cover. The handle moved, but the door
stayed closed. I swung the heavy barrel of the Colt into the
window and was showered by pellets of glass.

"I'll get out. I'll get out. Don't shoot!" the man inside
the car shouted.

I ignored his screams and came off the concrete
enough to put my elbow on the glassless window ledge.
The small white-haired man inside tried to slip out, but
my left hand found his throat, and I held him up. The
man gagged and went stiff; his pants became wet as he
pissed himself. Over the shoulder of the human shield,
and through the windshield, I saw Miller approaching
with the same two-handed police combat stance. Miller
hadn't seen me behind the man in the car. I aimed wide
and let three bullets go. The gunshots rang inside the car
and etched a network of spider webs into the windshield.
I let the white-haired man go, and he put his hands over
his ears, sobbing wordlessly with pain and fear. When I

came up from behind the car, Miller was out of his combat stance. He was hauling his fat ass back to his squad car and his radio.

I kept my head down and ran down the street. I made the first left and opened the door to the Volvo. I had left the car under the cover of a low-hanging tree. The branches covered the car like probing fingers, making it hard to see from more than three metres away. I reloaded the gun using bullets I had packed in the glove box — and kept my eye on the corner for Miller. I saw something else entirely. The third Chinese lookout, the blond, rounded the corner in his tight leather jacket. In his hand he held a black pistol.

Only two of the guards had made an appearance in the gunfight. That meant the third man ran either for cover or for a phone. The fact that he was here looking for me meant that he must have gone for the phone. A coward wouldn't follow someone who had put two of his associates down; he'd stay put and cook up a story. The blond man didn't let emotion or pride colour his actions. He let his friends get carved up in the street while he protected the front. He did what he was trained to do, and now he was making up for lost time. The blond was a pro who kept his head in a fight. That kind of man would get the make and plate of a car that sped away. I had to get out of the area before Miller's backup showed up and the whole neighbourhood was locked down. I also had to keep anyone else from putting me on their shit list. That meant the last sentry had to go.

I reached up, turned off the overhead light, then eased the door open. The blond guard had started down the middle of the street, gun in hand. He checked each car with a cautious lean from a safe distance. He never totally turned his back on anything he hadn't already checked. This guy was by the numbers and dangerous. I opened the car door wide and stepped behind the tree trunk.

The blond saw the door ten seconds later and slowly approached. I took the gun by the barrel and got ready to slip out from behind the tree. Too many gunshots had rung out; more from this direction would make it harder to slip away in the commotion and confusion. When the triggerman bent to look under the branches and into the car, I rolled out from behind the tree and closed the distance between us. The blond saw me coming at the last second. His gun was useless pointed inside the car, so he bent his head forward and turtled, trying to take the impact and stay conscious. The butt of the .45 glanced off the back of the Chinese man's head with enough force to send him to his knees. I pivoted and swung the gun down on his wrist, sending his pistol into the darkness of the Volvo. My elbow drove back towards his face, but a kick met me halfway. The kick connected with my knee and hyper-extended the joint. I staggered back, using the car to stay up before awkwardly lunging back in. The blond was off his feet coming to meet me.

Part of me expected kung fu. What I got was a boxer's stance and a haymaker starting somewhere near the blond's back pocket. I shuffled forward and erased the gap between us, making the haymaker ineffective. My hands took fistfuls of shirt and pulled him towards me. His hands were still set up for the haymaker when my forehead connected with the bridge of his nose. He grunted, and readjusted, sending an uppercut between my hands on his shirt. The punch grazed my chin, and my teeth cracked together. I was dazed, but I stayed in tight. Boxers need a certain distance to remain effective. Eliminate the distance and the referee separates you. When there's no ref, the boxer is left somewhere unfamiliar. I introduced the blond to the new place by pulling down on his shirt with my left hand. His head came forward into my right fist. My knuckles compressed the soft cartilage of his throat, creating a gag and then no sound at all. The blow interrupted the flow of air and startled the blond. The effect was visible from head to toe. He was no longer fighting me; his body was instead fighting for air. My left hand pulled him in again, but my right hand stayed away. My head collided with his nose again, and it flattened like a balloon deflating. His body bounced off mine, but my left arm reeled him back in. My elbow came across my body and caught the gasping face in the jaw. I didn't let his body fall, I shoved him into the car and got in behind him.

I drove out of the neighbourhood in the opposite direction of the commotion. Miller's call had gotten out fast, and the response was even faster. Ahead of me, I could see flashing lights; seconds later, I heard the sirens of the approaching police cars. I let my right foot sink to the floorboards and felt the Volvo purr in response as though the engine were thanking me for the chance to run head first at the police cars. The odometer hit seventy as I leaned across the seat and pushed the passenger door open. The emergency brake flatlined the odometer and sent the car into a long skid. I turned the wheel and released the brake, pulling out of the controlled 180. The blond's body hit the pavement and rolled. Each limb flailed out straight like spokes on a tire as the body tore down the street at ten over the speed limit. Eventually, the broken limbs made slow, fluid, limp arcs as the body careened to a stop on the asphalt.

The lights, now behind me, had a speed bump to deal with, and the cops inside had protocol to follow. Procedure dictated that they had to stop and help the body in the street before they followed in pursuit. The Volvo was already purring again as I made use of the diversion and wound around a corner to a side street. Two turns later, the sound of police sirens was barely audible as I drove away from the crime scene. I slowed the car down and became just another downtown car on its way out of the core.

CHAPTER FOURTEEN

I drove out to Igor's house but found the driveway empty. I parked the car and moved around the back of the house. All of the lights were off inside. Through the window, by the dim light given off by the digital displays on all of the appliances, I could see the burned and beaten dead body of Tatiana still on the floor.

Igor had a head start and nothing else to lose. Holding up the Secret Garden had been his fourth-quarter Hail Mary. The plan failed, and now there was no way he could recoup what he had lost. I needed to catch up with him before he went to see his boss. If he got there ahead of me, he would disappear without a trace, and so would my chances of keeping my face out of the news. I didn't know where Sergei Vidal operated, and I couldn't ask Morrison. After he heard about Miller getting shot at, his conscience would force him to come after me. Morrison was the type to bend the rules to get the job done, but no cop would let a murder attempt on one of their own go. I had to find Igor on my own.

I left the house and drove to my only other lead, the Steel City Lounge. I drove by the entrance and saw Igor's car double-parked out front. The car was empty, and the engine was still ticking. I did a drive around the neighbourhood to make sure Morrison wasn't still hanging around the club. His car was nowhere to be seen. I figured everyone played dumb when he first came to the club and he struck out. He wouldn't have wasted more time on a dead-end lead, he'd have decided to go after Igor another way.

I parked on a side street and waited under a burnt-out streetlight for the right moment to move. At 12:15 a.m., the street was bare. If Igor was watching his back, he'd see me coming. After twenty minutes, my patience was rewarded. A Hummer limousine pulled up out front and belched out a rowdy bachelor party. The groom had a jail-striped shirt on and a foam ball and chain around his ankle. The group chanted "Whores!" as they walked into the club. All of them were too drunk to notice that their party picked up one more member at the door. I broke from the party inside, took a corner table near the bar, and scanned the room for Igor. He wasn't hard to find.

The Russian was on stage screaming at one of the girls. The music still pumped as Igor's words put a look of terror onto the girl's face. Spit left his mouth as he screamed; it arced high in the stage lights before nose diving into the topless dancer's hair. The floor staff, each wearing a T-shirt with SECURITY printed on the back, all turned their backs to the stage. Igor ran the club, and they knew better than to try to control him; they focused their attention on the audience. The crowd, drunk and horny, did not know how to deal with the spectacle. Many turned their attention to another dancer or their drinks; others got excited. There was part of the crowd that liked watching the intimidation and humiliation of the girl on stage, and there was a murmur of appreciation from the men still watching. The groom from the bachelor party screamed, "Hell, yeah!"

He broke free from the party he was with and approached the stage.

"You tell that bitch, man."

Igor took a fistful of hair and pushed the stripper to her knees. He pointed to the pole she had used and screamed more words in her face. Igor backhanded the girl onto her ass, and the groom jumped. Both his hands were in the air, and he cheered loudly. I heard his hoot, over the bass, from my table. He clumsily pulled out a camera phone and held it high in the air as Igor slapped the girl again.

Igor's body blocked the groom's shot, so the fake jail-bird drunkenly climbed onto the stage for a better angle. He stumbled around Igor and forced the camera towards the girl's tear-stained face. Igor was surprised by the camera and even more by the presence of the man in the jail stripes on the stage with him.

The groom slapped Igor's back and nodded to him. Igor looked around the club, squinting to see beyond the stage lights. More people had looked away, trying to pretend the degradation on stage wasn't happening. The bachelor party at the bar was still all eyes, watching their captain. Igor slapped the camera away and sucker-punched the groom. His drunk body went down all at once, and Igor was on him. Igor mounted the groom's body and began pounding down onto his face. His fist jackhammered into flesh. At first, he just broke skin and bruised flesh, but each successive punch did more and more damage. Blood began to spurt into the brightly lit air on the stage. More and more of the fluid shot into the air like liquid rubies. As the groom's face gave way to becoming pulp, teeth skittered away from the limp body.

The bachelor party rushed past the floor security and hit the stage after the twenty-seventh punch. The groom was convulsing when a member of the bachelor party finally tackled Igor. A crowd formed around Igor on stage as everyone tried to get a shot in, but the VIP section upstairs was on stage before Igor got hurt. A brawl broke out between Igor's men and the bachelor party. The twenty-something kids were all completely shit-faced, unlike Igor's men, who were hardened toughs. Igor's men had been drinking all night, but alcohol was an everyday thing to these men. The booze only dulled them enough to silence any morality that might try to speak up. They weren't drunk; they were ice-cold numb.

The bachelor party was thrown off the stage one by one until none was left but the groom. Igor spat on the still shaking body and walked upstairs to the VIP lounge with his crew. The audience that had been ignoring Igor's abuse of the stripper had taken notice of the fight and cleared their chairs. Everyone was on their feet trying to stay clear of the men being thrown from the stage — no one wanted to be mistaken for a member of the bachelor party. The floor security did double duty holding the crowd back and dragging the bodies of the bachelor party out the door one by one. There were murmurs and scared looks from the faces in the crowd until a new dancer hit the stage. It was amazing how fast a new gyrating naked woman on stage lured the crowd back to their seats.

Upstairs, the lounge was comprised of black leather, chrome tables, and neon lighting. Igor and his men sat on the shiny leather couches watching the action below. The lights made their angry faces demonic and made the roped-off area look like a modern circle of Dante's *Inferno*. The hours that followed were full of binge drinking and sexual assault. Women went up the stairs with trays of drinks and ran back down with torn clothing. Igor screamed and yelled at the stage, and more than once he came close to falling over the railing to the floor below.

Igor left at three, opting to drive himself home. I followed him out and stood ten feet away while he tried repeatedly to open his door. Igor had lost everything: his girl, his money, his job, all of it was gone. What he hadn't lost yet was his usefulness. Igor could still get me off the hook with Morrison. He'd lost Sergei Vidal's money; Sergei would not let that slide. The day's grace Igor said he needed was three hours over. Igor was late, and now Sergei would come collecting. I had worked for a mob boss for a long time. Money drives every action, and pride keeps everything in line. Igor had fucked with both. It would be time to pay up very soon.

Igor got home in one piece. His tires dragged against the curb more than ten times, and he dinged the side mirrors of a whole row of cars on a side street, but he survived the trip. He parked diagonally in the driveway and walked towards the house, making only two detours into the flowerbeds before he managed to get to the door. Covered in dirt, Igor managed to fall into the open doorway.

I parked across the street and watched the house. No lights came on, and no curtains moved. I gave Igor five minutes before I opened the trunk and pulled out the cash I stole off him the night before.

I lugged the bag across the street and let it rest beside the front door. I unholstered the .45 and took out the house keys I'd stolen from the kitchen drawer earlier. I used my left hand to quietly ease the key into the lock. I turned the key to the right, but the mechanism offered no resistance — Igor had left the door unlocked. I crept inside, letting the black eye of the .45 lead the way. Tatiana was still in the kitchen, and Igor was nowhere in sight. I covered the first floor and then moved up the stairs. The second step responded to my weight with a groan, so I put my next step closer to the wall. The wood was more stable there. Halfway up, I saw a black shoe dangling over the edge. At the top of the stairs, I saw that Igor had done my work for me; he was sprawled out on his stomach — unconscious. His chest rose and fell at a regular rate, and his mouth pushed out puffs of air in measured gusts. Igor was alive, for now.

I went back down the stairs, opened the door, and pulled the duffel bag inside. I put the bag on the welcome mat and quietly unzipped the double zipper. I took eight of the paper-bound bundles of cash and walked into the kitchen. I ripped the bands and spread the money over the kitchen table, the counters, the floor, and Tatiana's body. The bills landed on her blistered face and lay on top of the crusted blood. I took the rest of the money into the basement and used an old chair to stand on while I pushed free some of the ceiling tiles. When there was enough space, I put the bag up in the ceiling. The weight of the bag pushed some of the other tiles out of place and made an obvious lump in the ceiling. I left the chair in place below the money and walked back upstairs. Igor never stirred when I opened the door — he was dead to the world, just the way the rest of the planet wanted him.

I slid back behind the wheel of the car and got comfortable. Igor had been drugged and then had gone on his own bender — he would sleep for a while. I dry chewed more caffeine pills and chased them with warm soda while I watched the house. My plan would only work if the Russians responded in the same way every other gangster I'd worked with would have.

At 9:30 a.m., a black Hummer pulled to the curb in front of Igor's house. The windows were too tinted for me to see inside, but I knew whoever was inside worked for Sergei Vidal. I memorized the plate while I waited for something to happen. Both the driver and passenger side doors opened, and I saw that I was right. Nikolai and Pietro, Nick and Pete, Sergei's personal security, got out. They looked around the neighbourhood before taking a step away from the cover of the vehicle. They were not anywhere as big as the man they had replaced. Ivan had been six and a half feet tall and at least 300 pounds of beef. These men were unlike Ivan; they were compact — five-ten, maybe 200 pounds. They had bodies built in the military. Running with heavy packs and relentless days of body weight exercises had left the men with hard, wiry physiques. They would be fast, tough, and relentless — like wolves. Wolves weren't large, that would conflict with their purpose. Wolves hunted prey almost twice their size, and they always came home with dinner. They ran their prey down in relentless pursuit, then hit them where they were weak. These two men had the same feral look I saw every time I looked in the mirror.

The military campaigns in Afghanistan would be a problem. You shoot at some corner thug, he runs. Maybe he shoots back at you over his shoulder as he goes. Army is different. Combat veterans don't lose their heads, and they don't run unless there is a tactical reason for it. They will take cover and shoot back, and not over their shoulders. Most of the veterans who took a job in the streets were adrenaline junkies who got spoiled in the service. Pulling the trigger for a paycheque was a high they couldn't shake, and normal life didn't have an equivalent.

The blond, Nick, unholstered a gun and held it against his thigh between the Hummer and his leg, while Pete walked to the door. The light reflected off Pete's scalp as he crossed the driveway. His hair was shaved so short that it was hard to tell what colour it was without squinting. He kept a hand behind his back while he peeked in the darkened windows. He finally tried the doorknob, and when it worked he motioned Nick over with a single hand gesture. Nick hid the gun inside his leather coat and walked up the driveway. On the porch both men looked around one more time before drawing their guns and nodding their heads.

The two men entered the house in a professional two-man formation keeping their shit tight. Their guns went up in two-handed grips, and Pete went in straight. Nick followed, covering Pete before angling off to check the front room. I saw Nick cross the doorway, and then the door closed. I pulled the Colt from my shoulder holster and put it in my lap. Igor had never noticed me parked across the street, but he sucked. Nick and Pete might have caught sight of me from the tinted Hummer. They could have decided to scout me out from the house and use the back door to come at me from a spot I wasn't watching. I rolled down the window and slouched in the seat, making as small a target as possible. No bullets came. Instead, Nick and Pete came out the front door with Igor. Both had a hand on a shoulder, and Igor's face was bloody — Nick and Pete had asked some questions with their hands. Igor didn't struggle, he just got into the back seat with Pete. Nick threw a grocery bag into the front seat and got in. I figured the bag had some of the money I'd spread around the kitchen.

The Hummer slipped away from the curb and headed into the city. I gave the boxy vehicle a head start, but I kept it in sight as I followed behind.

Morrison's CI's had done their job. Sergei Vidal heard through his twisted grapevine that Igor was stealing, and the proof came when he was late with the money. Sergei had sent his two best to pick up Igor — that meant Sergei was focused. I had come across Sergei's focus once before in an office building belonging to a bunch of computer programmers. In broad daylight, in a crowded neighbourhood, Sergei sent a crew to execute more than ten men and women. He sent his right hand after the most important man in the office. Everything would have gone down according to plan if I hadn't gotten there first. I put a bullet in Sergei's right-hand man, three more a day later. I didn't deal with the rest of Sergei, and now he was back with two new right hands.

They worked fast and by the numbers. There was no sloppiness or rust on Nick or Pete. Whatever Russian military outfit they bounced out of left them with good habits. Good habits made moving on Sergei tough — not impossible, just tough.

We drove down Main Street until it turned into King. We kept on King going out of Hamilton into Stoney Creek. Stoney Creek was famous for ice cream from the Stoney Creek Dairy and for a battlefield where some soldiers mixed it up during the War of 1812. Around these sights, a town for the upper middle class sprang up. The town was an appendage of Hamilton. If Hamilton was a diseased body, Stoney Creek was the manicured hand.

The Hummer stayed on King until it pulled across traffic to the curb in front of an off-track betting building. I kept my distance, double-parking a couple hundred metres down the street. It was just later than a quarter after ten, and the Jackpot OTB looked closed; its patio was empty, and the white plastic outdoor chairs were still up on the tables. Nick and Pete got out of the Hummer, bringing the money and Igor with them. Nick and Pete stopped at the door. Both men scanned the street with their arms just inside their jackets. Satisfied with what they saw, Nick pulled the door open and ushered Igor inside. I drove past the OTB, circled back, and parked across the street.

Inside the OTB would be at least five people plus Igor. Nick and Pete I saw, but Sergei would have two others at least. They weren't going to kill Igor right away; if they wanted him dead, it would have happened at his house. They brought him back because they were told to do so. When Sergei saw the money, he would send men back to find the rest. They would tear the house apart until they found what I left in the ceiling. Once the money was recovered, Sergei would have Igor killed and disposed of. It would always be money first, blood second.

I pulled out my cell phone and dialled a number I knew never changed. When I finished my call, I called another number I heard on the radio the day before. I was dialling a number I could see on a sign a block down the road when two different men left the OTB. I spoke into the phone as I watched them get into a Cadillac sedan and drive away. The two men were in suits. The jackets looked to be a size bigger than the pants, probably to conceal the weapons underneath. Muscle often never thought about tailoring a coat to conceal a gun the way I had done — they just wore bigger clothes. The two men were not like Nick and Pete. Their bodies weren't the same; these men had the bodies of bruisers. Each had to be 250 pounds of muscle. The Cadillac seemed to wince as they got inside and began adjusting the mirrors and seats. Both men were bald by choice; they had shaven their heads completely, leaving nothing but razor burn and glare. Most would think that the two huge men were Sergei's security, but I knew better. The two bruisers were like guard dogs — big and scary animals who kept most people away. Nick and Pete, the real killers, looked nothing like those men, but that was the point. They were sleek like matadors — they let you get in close before they drove the sword home.

I finished my call, then dialled Detective Sergeant Huata Morrison's private number, the one left on the back of his card. He picked up right away but said nothing. I listened to the silence and matched his with my own.

"What do you want?" he asked.

I let a bit more of the silence run down his battery before answering. "It's time to move."

"No."

"No?"

"We're done," he said. "You went too far, and now we're done."

"What happened?" I asked, knowing the response.

"What happened? What happened is you took a shot at a cop, that's what happened."

"What are you talking about?" I lied.

"Enough! You thought you could play me with all of your lies, and I'm telling you it's done. You're done."

"What cop got shot at?"

Silence answered me.

"Morrison, I can prove to you I didn't do it — just tell me what cop it was."

"Miller," he said. It sounded like it came out through clenched teeth.

"When?"

"Last night." I heard teeth grinding in my ear.

"Where?"

"Outside some restaurant downtown, the Secret Garden. Like the fucking Springsteen song."

"And why do you think it was me?"

"You got a hard on for Miller, and we both know it. You asked about him too many times for you not to be involved."

"You know what the Secret Garden is?" I asked.

"A shit restaurant and a bad fucking song."

"It's a front for the Fat Cobra Society. Their drug money goes through it."

I got no answer.

"Why was Miller there?"

Still no answer, so I repeated the question.

"Traffic stop," Morrison said.

"That normal for the Lieutenant? Pulling traffic stops? Or did he just feel like going above and beyond the job yesterday because that is the kind of outstanding cop he is? He can't let even the smallest infractions to the law go? Was this upholding of the law a day or night event?"

"Night."

"Miller work nights in the city a lot?"

Silence answered me.

"So you got Miller doing a traffic stop at night, in the city, outside a Chinese drug front, and you think I shot at him? You think I'm dumb enough to make enemies of the Chinese *and* the cops? You're a fucking detective, look at the facts and detect something from them. 'Cause if it looks like fire and smells like fire, it's probably a fat crooked cop."

"Why did you call?" Morrison asked.

"We made a deal. I'm giving you something, but you'll need to do some detecting. Can you handle that, Columbo?"

"Tell me."

"I told you about a name — Igor."

"I remember."

"You need to get to his place right now. It's right by . . ."

"Bayfront Park," he said, finishing my sentence. "I'll know the place because there will be a yellow car parked out front."

Morrison was even faster than I had thought he was.

MIKE KNOWLES

He was stalking me using the one clue I let slip, and he was now just a step behind. If I had taken any longer, he would have found me staking out Igor's house. Then the game would have changed to something bloodier. "You've been there?" I asked, knowing he hadn't.

"I just found out about his house last night. I planned to go there today."

"You need to get there now. Inside you'll find two men, drug money, and a body. If you put your thinking cap on, Holmes, you might get a good lead out of the two men." I hung up the phone and looked at the man approaching the OTB with his arms full. The pizza I had ordered was right on time.

CHAPTER FIFTEEN

The Pizza Pizza delivery guy showed up eighteen minutes after I called with three sets of twins and an order of wings. Sergei was on the hook for $78.34. It took two minutes for the body of the delivery guy to come bouncing out the door. Nick had thrown him out with one hand; the other held a slice of pizza.

Pete threw the full boxes of pizza and wings at the delivery guy and walked back inside with Nick. The pizza guy picked himself up, flipped off the window, and walked away from the mess on the sidewalk. He made it three steps away before Nick was outside again. He screamed at the delivery guy and started towards him. The pizza guy put two hands up in appeasement and walked back with his head low to clean up the mess. He worked fast under the watchful eye and foot of Nick.

The mess was gone, and Nick was back inside when Pizza Hut arrived with ten medium pizzas. Sergei owed $124.18 to the Hut and its teenaged, acne-scarred, red-hat collection agency. The kid didn't even get in the door. Nick and Pete opened the frosted glass door before he could put down the pizza and open it himself. The door came at the kid fast, and it knocked him on his ass and sent pizza everywhere.

I had the window down just enough to hear the commotion.

"Who sent you here?" Nick demanded. He had an accent that was unmistakably Russian. "Who?"

The kid crab-walked back from the door and the blond man, scrambling to get to his feet. Pete passed Nick and planted his right foot on the kid's chest. The kid fought against the foot, but Pete just put more weight on him. The kid gave up and fell to the pavement, cracking his head.

Nick picked up each box and lifted the flap. When all he found was pizza, a rain of bread, cheese, and sauce fell on the kid. This happened nine times. Nick pulled a slice from the last box and let the cardboard fall to the ground. He told the kid to clean his shit up, and the kid nodded as best he could while still cradling the back of his head. The crack against the pavement had cut deep, and blood seeped through his hair and fingers. Nick and Pete went back inside, leaving the kid to clean up the mess one-handed. When he left, his hands and shirt were red from the sauce and the blood. I could see his confusion as he looked from hand to shirt trying to figure out how much blood he had lost. He stumbled away never knowing what was his and what belonged to Pizza Hut or why he had to give up either to the pavement.

By the dashboard clock, it was eight minutes until Domino's showed up. This time it wasn't an acne-speckled kid, it was a middle-aged man with a thick moustache. He wore a light blue golf shirt adorned with black-and-white checkerboard sleeves, navy shorts that gave everyone a view of his inner thigh hair, and old Velcro-strap running

MIKE KNOWLES

shoes. The untrimmed moustache, the clothes, the shitty job all led me to believe that this was a guy who was a joke to everyone he met. He wasn't in on the joke, and he never would be. Worse, he was in front of a door that led to two men with zero sense of humour.

Fortune smiled on the man with the moustache. Nick and Pete met him at the door and told him "No" too many times to count. The delivery guy pointed to his receipt, proving that he was in the right, but Nick and Pete didn't move. They shook their heads until Nick exploded in moustache's face. He screamed, "No, not ours! Now get the fuck out of here!"

The delivery guy saw the Russian was serious and backed away. Nick and Pete didn't watch him go like they did with the others, they just turned their backs and went inside.

I got out of the car and caught up to the Domino's guy on the street. The thirty bucks in my fist would cover the $24.18 bill with enough for a good tip.

"Hey! Hey, Domino's!"

He turned to face me, and I put on what I guessed to be my best apologetic face.

"I'm sorry about the boys. We bring a lot of cash in in the mornings, and they get too protective sometimes."

"They didn't have to yell. I don't appreciate being yelled at. I wanted to work things out, but they wouldn't let me speak. That's not how you treat a delivery guy. I just go where they tell me. When people don't pay, I gotta prove it was a crank call, or my boss will think I screwed up. Then I gotta eat the cost myself."

"Let me make it up to you," I said, showing him the money. "I'll take the pizza. How much is it?"

Domino's looked around. "We're not really supposed to do it this way. Store policy is very clear. I'm not supposed to sell the pizza on the street. Business should only be transacted at the customer's place of work or business."

"We can go back to the store if you want. I'm sure the boys will be nicer this time."

He thought about it for a second. "No, no, no. I'm just saying for next time. Next time you should pay at the door. It'll be twenty-four eighteen."

I gave him the thirty dollars and told him to keep the change. I waved him goodbye and watched him get into his Ford Taurus. When he was out of sight, I put two of the boxes down and pulled the .45 from my jacket. I zipped up the coat so my shoulder rig was invisible and put one of the pizza boxes over the gun. The Colt was in my hand, under the flat bottom of the box, invisible from view so long as I kept the box tilted forward.

I left the other two boxes on the ground and walked, bill in hand, towards the OTB. I didn't just walk straight up to the front door — that had gone badly for the three other delivery men. Nick and Pete saw them coming and never let them get inside. I waited for a few minutes, three stores down, until a city bus came down the street. Traffic was slow enough that the bus crept along the street in the right lane. When the light turned red, the bus blocked the OTB's view from at least half of its windows. I walked into traffic along the side of the bus facing away from the storefront and hooked around the back bumper jogging as though I was trying to cross the street before the light turned. I rounded the front of the bus and jogged straight in the front entrance.

I got five steps inside before Nick and Pete blocked my way. The OTB had an area with several windows for business as well as a bar surrounded by tables underneath huge mounted flat-screen televisions. This wasn't a walk in, walk out, kind of place; it was a gambler's paradise.

"No, no, no, no. No pizza. We order nothing. Leave

now!" Nick yelled. Pete said nothing.

"Whoa, whoa, guys. Let's look at the order," I said, pulling out the Domino's bill. "One medium pizza for Igor."

"No pizza. No!" Nick screamed. His breath was warm in my face.

"Igor?" Pete asked. I marked him as the smart one, Nick as the violent one. Nick looked at him, confused, then looked back at me after he figured it out. "Did you say Igor?"

I checked the bill and nodded at Pete.

"Who told you that name?"

"No one told me anything — it's on the bill along with the cost. You owe me thirteen forty-nine."

Nick closed the distance between us, taking over the conversation again, ready for violence. "You will tell me who told you that name." He slapped the pizza box, trying to knock it out of my hands, but it didn't fall. He grabbed the box and tried to wrestle it away from me, but it stayed in my hands. We locked eyes for a second as he groped for the pizza and I grinned; Nick didn't understand. He got it a second later when the .45 took his knee off his leg.

The big slug scrambled patella and cartilage and sent Nick to the floor. His scream was silent at first, but he found his voice fast. I turned on Pete, but he was already running towards the bar. Pete didn't waste any emotion on his partner. He was surviving, just like he had been trained to do.

The .45 spat loud, obscene shots at him, but they all came up wide. Each spasm of the gun was just a little off. Pete jerked up, down, left, right, making him a hard target. He threw himself over the bar, and I moved in his wake. I heard the metallic crunch of a shotgun loading. Pete came up with the shotgun levelled at his shoulder ready to shoot through whatever cover I took, but I wasn't where he thought I was. I was like him — a survivor. I had been shot at before, and it didn't spook me anymore. It scared me as much as it always did, but I stored the fear away while I worked. The .45 was in my hands, three metres away from where I had been standing when Pete went for cover. Pete caught sight of me, out of the corner of his eye, and realized that he had misjudged where I would be. He turned at the hips to correct his aim as I pulled the trigger. The first bullet hit Pete in the left shoulder, spinning him and the shotgun away from me. The second shot punched a dark hole into his back. Red hit the bottles behind the bar as the lead ripped through the wiry flesh. Pete went down behind the bar, and I heard the shotgun hit the floor, I heard it for a second, then a bullet ripped through my right ear.

I dove left and hit the floor hard. The wind went out of me as I hit the floor rolling. A second bullet whizzed over my head from Nick's direction. Pete had moved so fast that I never got the chance to put Nick all the way out. I crawled behind the bar and saw Pete's prone body. He had managed to roll himself over. His hands covered the hole in his shoulder and the exit wound on the front of his body. I crouch-walked closer and pulled a pistol from his belt — a 9mm Heckler and Koch USP. I put the gun in my coat pocket and kept moving.

"He is hard to kill," Pete said to me, nodding over the bar towards Nick.

"Aren't we all."

I grabbed one of the bottles that hit the floor when I shot Pete and lobbed it over the bar. It landed with a crash. I lobbed a second and a third. With the third bottle came a grunt — I knew where Nick was. I picked up the twelve-gauge Mossberg and put my back against the wall. I put five more bottles in the air; each landed with a crash near the spot that produced the grunt. As the fifth bottle left my hand, I stood with the Mossberg and pulled the trigger. I racked the slide and shot again as I stepped away from the bar. The bottles I had thrown landed near the dining area where Nick had taken cover. The shotgun was aimed low, and it caught the edge of a table and the back of a chair as it let loose. None of the spray from the shotgun caught Nick; he had sensed what was coming after the bottles and had managed to drag his mangled leg across the floor. The barrel of the Mossberg followed the trail of blood on the floor towards the booths on the wall where Nick had taken cover from the bottles. Nick had burrowed in like a tick behind the vinyl in a spot that might have offered him a chance at surprising me if there wasn't a crimson trail ratting him out. I racked the slide again and shot at the furniture hiding Nick from me. The twelve gauge punched a hole through the back of the booth and toppled the table.

"Okay, okay," Nick screamed.

I put another shot in Nick's direction.

"Stop!"

Two hands came up from behind the aerated seat, empty. I walked towards Nick and saw a matching H and K pistol two feet away from his body. His face was pale under his sweaty blond mop.

"Put your hands on your leg before you bleed out," I said.

Nick nodded and sat up. He groaned with the effort and screamed when he put his hands to his leg. His eyes were looking glassy, and I figured shock was setting in. He didn't even flinch when I put the butt of the shotgun between his eyes.

The OTB was suddenly quiet. I looked at my jacket

and saw blood soaked into the sleeve. I took a handful of napkins from a dispenser on one of the tables still upright and put them to my ear. The sting took me by surprise, and I closed my eyes for a second. My ear didn't feel right under the napkins — the lobe hung too low. The napkins came away red and damp, so I pressed them harder to the side of my head again. I managed to pack the tissue paper around my ear, using the blood to hold the thin white material to my head. The rest of the napkins were used to wipe down my coat. The waterproof material kept the blood from absorbing, and the napkins soaked up the beaded fluid and became heavy. I put the napkins in my pocket and took the shotgun down a single hallway leading away from the betting windows and bar. At the end of the hallway was a small backroom with an office and an emergency exit. The exit had a sticker on the door explaining that if opened the mechanism would set off an alarm. The deafening silence told me that no one had used the door.

The office door was closed, and when I tried the lock I found the handle didn't move. I crossed to the other side of the door, closer to the exit, and knocked. No one answered.

"Nikolai and Pietro are down and bleeding to death as I speak."

"I care not," a voice I remembered as belonging to Sergei Vidal said.

"See if this makes you care. I got the shotgun from behind the bar in my hands. You don't give me what I want, I'm going to fire through the walls. Twelve gauge like this should spread enough to pulp everything. You know what pulp means, Sergei?"

"I know pulp. What do you want?"

"Send Igor out. That's all. Send him out, and we leave."

I heard a hushed conversation and a few loud "No's"

from Igor. I racked the slide on the gun for effect and let a shotgun shell fall to the concrete floor.

"Ten seconds, Sergei, then I just let the shotgun sort it out."

"Nine, eight, seven, six, five . . ." I shouldered the gun and got ready. If I bluffed once, Sergei would find a way to exploit it. At three, the door opened, and Igor walked out with his hands up. When Igor was beside me, I pulled him away from the doorway. I looped the shotgun under his chin and snaked my left arm around the barrel. My left hand found the back of Igor's head, and the choke compressed. The hard metal gun on Igor's throat clamped his carotid artery, and blood stopped flowing to Igor's brain. Igor left his feet as I arched my back. Eight seconds later, he was unconscious.

"Set-up was just like you said, boss. Let's get you out of here," I said to Igor as he went limp, loud enough for Sergei to hear. I shouldered him quietly and kicked open the back door. The alarm screeched to life as my feet touched the alley gravel. I hustled Igor around the corner and onto a side street that connected with King. I was on the busy street in thirty seconds and in the car thirty seconds after that. I wasn't worried about Sergei following me; he had to get the alarm off before someone showed up and found the bodies in the OTB. I didn't kill Nick and Pete, because live bodies present more problems than dead ones. Dead bodies get carted off, buried, and erased. Wounded men, if they are found by the authorities, go to hospitals and get questioned. Nick and Pete would never talk to the cops, but they would still bring all kinds of heat down on Sergei unless they were dealt with quietly. Sergei couldn't outsource this problem to anyone else — there was no time. If Sergei wanted to stay out of custody, he would have to do something about his men — and that meant giving me time to get away.

Within the hour, Igor was taped to a chair in the motel room next to mine. His clothes were in the bathroom, and the folding knife was in my hand.

MIKE KNOWLES

The bullet had torn through the lower half of my ear, leaving a section of undamaged ear hanging. I used the knife in the bathroom to take the wrecked part of the ear off. It took two rolls of toilet paper to stop the bleeding and a piece of duct tape over some more of the cheap motel toilet paper to cover the wound.

The motel room next to mine was just as tight. Igor's chair was at the foot of the bed, and it took up all the space between the bed and the wall. To get behind Igor required a trip over the mattress. His feet were taped to the back two legs, and his wrists were fastened to the metal frame behind his back. Over his mouth, a piece of tape kept him quiet. His eyes weren't on me, they were on the knife.

"Feels like we've been here before, eh? Except last time you had *me* tied down."

Igor thrashed his head, the only part of his body that he could move, and grunted at me.

"I've been reading *I'm Okay, You're Okay*." Igor's eyes peeled away from the knife and found mine. "I figure you thought of your own solution to get that closure you wanted. One that wasn't in the book. You figured I'm not okay, and neither are you. But you thought that if you killed me you could get okay. Sort of take out half of the equation, and everything will sort itself out." I chuckled. The sound made Igor's lip quiver under the tape. "I hate to break it to you, Igor, but killing never sorts anybody out. If anything, it turns you inside out even more. The more you do it the less it will help, because you keep turning off a bit more of yourself. It's like burning nerve endings one at a time. You feel it for a minute while it dies, but pretty soon you can't feel anything no matter how hard you try. Way I see it, you got it all wrong. We'll never be okay. Okay isn't for people like us. We've done too much wrong to too many people. Okay went out the window the first night you rode with a gun in your pocket and violence in your heart. You can never come back from that. The most you can hope for is alive. It's not what we deserve for what we've done, but it's what we get. It's all doing wrong earns you, if you're good enough at the bad. That was always your problem. Try as you might, you never had the gravel in your guts, but somehow you managed to defy the odds and stay above ground. Now stay put."

I went outside and walked into my room. I powered up the cell phone and dialled Morrison while I cut through the decades-old yellowed drywall with the knife. I winced when the phone touched the ear damaged by Nick's bullet and quickly switched the cell to the other side of my face. Morrison picked up as I finished my first cut into the wall.

"Morrison."

I dragged the knife a foot down the wall, turned the blade, and made another long cut. "Where are you?"

"The house you told me about. It's a fucking mess."

"You having crime scene techs go through it?" I turned the knife again and started a cut back up the wall.

"No, I got some uniforms with some mops. They're just gonna wring 'em out back at the lab."

"Not all of the blood belongs to the girl; some of it belongs to Igor. If you compare it to the blood left on the bed in the hospital, you will find a match."

"He good for it?"

"I didn't kill the nurse. He was the last one to see her alive. Either he did it or the girl did after she let him loose. She was a hard one; don't let the skinny legs fool you."

"This is a start, but where's Igor?" said Morrison. "I have to have someone to tie all this blood to."

"He's in the wind, but I'll have him soon," I said. "What happened with the two men on the scene?"

"We found them in the bedroom fucking with the mattress. Put a big slit down the centre. They don't speak English though. Only word they seemed to have a grasp of was 'lawyer.' That was one word they knew real well."

"You know who they are?"

"I know they're Russians."

"They work for Sergei Vidal."

"No shit."

"No shit," I said.

"Why were they here?"

"You're the detective. I'm sure you can piece together a motive if you put your mind to it," I said as I put the phone on my shoulder so I could use both of my hands to pull the drywall free.

"So," Morrison said, "I have Sergei Vidal's men at the site of a brutal slaying with shit thrown all over the house like someone was searching for something. Something they didn't find yet, because there was nothing in the car or on them. What am I gonna find in the house?"

I ignored the question. "Is Miller there?"

"Why?"

"I want you to tell him something."

"I told you he's clean," Morrison said, still clinging to his badge brother.

"Why do you stick up for him when you know he's dirty?"

"And how do I know that? Because you told me? You think your word means anything to me? I know your type — I've been schooled on people like you since birth. My brother is like you. He's a meth addict 'cept back home on the island we don't call it meth. We call it P. He's twelve years older than me, so he was my idol growing up. Problem was he lied all the time so he could get high. He'd say we'd go to the park after school, but he'd never come get me because he was high. He'd tell me we'd go to a rugby game, but I would sit home all night in my jersey because he went and got high. When he got worse, he'd steal from me to get high. He stole my bike, my Nintendo, one time he sold my new shoes. Every time he came down he'd swear it would never happen again, but it would because he was a junkie, and lying is part of being a junkie. See, to me, you're just like him. You'll say anything you can to get what you want, but it will always be a lie because you're a junkie just like him."

I pulled some cheap insulation out of the wall and dropped it on the floor. The other wall of Igor's room was now visible through the square hole I'd made.

"You're not on P like my brother, you're a criminal addicted to something stronger than meth; something much more addictive — staying out of jail. I don't really need to explain to you how hooked you are on staying out of a cage, do I? It's only been a few days since I turned you loose, and you've already killed a man with my gun and blackmailed me with it to avoid doing time. What other things have you done, that I don't know about, to get your fix? Who else had to die so you could walk the streets?"

"Let's cut the shit. You and I are both bent. You set me loose, Morrison. Everything that happened was because you saw fit to use me as bait. And what was I on the hook for? You just wanted a bust you could attach your name to so you could get ahead, so don't try to pretend that you're Dudley Do-Right. You're just an opportunist with a badge — a different kind of junkie who gets off on his pay grade."

"You're right about that, mate. There's definitely some dirt under my fingernails. Most cops are a little dirty. No one trusts a guy who doesn't have a little stink on him. And maybe Miller has dirtier hands than me, but I'm not turning on him on your say so. I know you're running game, mate, I've been lied to by better, and it won't work."

"Maybe I am wrong about Miller," I said. "But you set me loose to shake the trees. You wanted me to find you a bigger fish to arrest, and now you're changing the rules because the fish I found stinks. You need to get okay with what I have because there is nothing else on the menu. You want a big bust with a lot of press? Then you need to accept that Miller is involved in some way. Deep down you know I'm right. You have to admit, things just seem to have a habit of happening when he's around."

Morrison sighed. "Yeah," he said. "They do." He paused, and I heard him taking a deep breath. He let it out slowly, then said, "What do you want me to tell him?"

"You just tell him that Sergei is taking a run at Igor. Tell him that you heard it from a couple of your sources on the street while you were looking for Igor. Tell him Sergei almost got him, and you're sure that Igor will be turning up

dead any day now. Tell him your CI's are saying that whoever brings Igor in will be set for life. Get that? Set for life."

"Is it true?"

"Enough of it is."

Morrison sighed and told me he'd pass it along.

"You need to do it fast," I said.

"He's been hanging around for the last hour. He's real
interested in the scene. I'll tell him now."

"How did it end with your brother?" I asked.

Morrison paused, and when I heard his voice again it
was serious. "I arrested him the day I became a cop, and I
broke his arms so he couldn't shoot up anymore."

I hung up and listened with a motel glass against the
single sheet of drywall separating me and Igor. I could hear
him grunting clearly enough, then I heard a crash. I walked
back inside the other room, gun in hand, and found Igor
toppled in his chair. He had rocked back and forth too
hard and had sent the chair over on its back. I righted the
chair and rested the blade of the folding knife between
Igor's legs. I understood Igor. He worked out of a strip
club, kept a woman he never touched, and beat her regu-
larly because he was emasculated. Everything he did was
meant to seize some part of the masculinity he felt he was
lacking inside. Igor was empty, but he still had the right
useless decorations. I slid the knife forward until it met
resistance. His head thrashed, but the rest of him stayed
frozen. Igor couldn't afford to move because of the knife
against his balls.

"Igor," I said. His eyes were shut tight. I pushed harder
and said it again, "Igor." He looked at me, and I leaned in
closer. "You're already a fucking joke. Everyone sees through
you. Those who don't think you're gay. What will they say
when they find out you have no balls? Will they still let you
run the strip club if they know you can't enjoy it?"

Hitting Igor where it hurt was never going to be physical. If I cut him, he would give up and accept death. If I pierced something inside, something deep and emotional that was already rotten and festered, I would have him.

"You can get out of this, Igor." I showed him the red knife. "You want out?"

Igor nodded vigorously.

"All you have to do is make a call and say what I tell you to say. One call and we're done. Sound good?"

Igor nodded.

"Stay put."

I sat on the bed and wrote out what Igor was to say on the inside of a red palm Bible left inside the night stand. When I finished, I capped the pen and got Igor's cell phone out of his pants on the floor. I powered the phone up, pulled the tape on Igor's mouth free in one pull, and asked, "What's Miller's number?"

Igor looked at me puzzled for a moment. "Miller?"

"This isn't about you, Igor. You're just too stupid to realize that."

"I'm not stupid."

"Then tell me the number."

Igor told me, and I dialled. I put the phone between his shoulder and ear and rested the knife back against his balls. Igor grunted and then started reading.

"It's me. Listen, I'm in some shit, but I can bring it around. I just need some help. Sergei's trying to fuck me, and nothing can make that change, so I'm gonna fuck with him first. I'm gonna give you some places that he uses, dirty places. You're gonna bust 'em. You'll have enough to take down Sergei, then I'll take over."

I pulled the phone a few inches away from his ear so I could listen to Miller backpedal. He wanted no part in taking on Sergei. I had prepared for this.

Igor read on, "If I have to take you down with Sergei, I will. Remember, I have tapes, you cocksucker. I want you at the Escarpment Motel, Room Thirteen, in one hour, or we're done."

I took the phone off Igor, hit end, and closed the knife.

"That plan — it will never work," Igor grunted. "Miller will not help me go up against Sergei — it's suicide."

I nodded.

"You son of a bitch cocksucker. I am bait? You want Miller to tell Sergei so he can kill me. You motherfucker!"

Igor was getting loud, so I shut him up with a right hook. I didn't put much into the punch, just enough to feel teeth break. Igor spat blood on the floor and kept his voice down. "How did you know about the tapes I had on Miller?"

"I heard you tell him about them."

"When?"

"Right after you killed Tatiana in your kitchen."

Igor's mouth hung open. "You did this? All of this? You were the one in the street. You stole the money and shot at me in the restaurant. This is all your fault. You cocksucker, I'm going to . . ."

My fist hit Igor on the side of his rib cage on a spot where there was no muscle protecting the bones. This time I didn't hold back. His body, taped to the chair, went rigid with the impact, leaving the other side open for the same treatment. I felt bones break against my fist once then twice.

"Igor, you did this, not me. You opened up something that was dead because you couldn't let what happened go. Getting shot warped you when it should have just taught you something. You want to live in this life, you have to accept the risks. You want to live by the gun, you have to expect to die by the bullet."

Igor didn't answer me; his ribs were broken on both sides. Moving was agony and would be almost impossible. He forced out a few words in an almost soundless whisper. "You're dead, Moriarty."

I understood the threat. He would never be able to understand my response. I grinned at his fluttering eyes. "I'm not dead, Igor; I barely even exist. Death doesn't know my name, but he keeps searching for me, and I keep moving. I know he'll catch up one day; just not today. Today is your day."

I put him the rest of the way out with a fist and then untaped his wrists and ankles. The ribs would confine Igor to the bed. He'd barely be able to breathe enough to stand, let alone run. I left Igor's pistol on the corner of the night table just out of reach from the bed, propped Sergei's shotgun in the corner, and called Morrison.

"Miller leave?"

"Yeah. He got a call and took off."

"You free?"

"I can be, mate."

"Get in the car and drive to Whitney Billiards. It's near a restaurant in the West End called Greece on King."

"I know it."

"Get there and leave your phone on."

I hung up on Morrison and went to my own room. Everything was in motion now. What I cooked up would either work out or end in a bloodbath.

CHAPTER SEVENTEEN

The thin mattress in the room had two guns on it. The Glock police pistol, already on the hook for a murder, and the Colt .45. I wiped the guns down, making sure to get everything, even the brass cartridges. I didn't want to leave anything behind. I put the Colt in the shoulder rig and the Glock behind my back. I had to be careful about which gun I fired and at who. One wrong bullet would destroy any hopes I had of walking away.

I tore a piece of thin pillowcase off and wiped down every surface in the room. I put the rag in my pocket, turned off all of the lights, and stood by the door using the peephole to watch the parking lot. Time went by, and every few minutes I moved from the door to the hole in the drywall. Igor made no sounds at all from next door.

Eventually, an unmarked police cruiser rolled past the peephole, parked in the rear corner, and killed its engine. No one got out of the car. The bedside clock had only counted thirty-five minutes since I hung up Igor's phone. In the dark car across the lot, I saw the flare of a lighter, then the small circle of a cigarette. I knew it could go two ways with Miller. He could decide to kill Igor himself in an "attempted" arrest, earning himself a commendation, or he could trade up by selling Igor out to Sergei Vidal. I bet Miller wasn't going to try to kill Igor in an arrest attempt. There was too much chance an investigation into Igor might turn up his name or Igor's tapes. It would be better if Miller took care of Igor off the books. And if he was already freelancing, why not trade up for a better partner? Miller was corrupt already; why should he settle for being in bed with mid-level muscle when he could get in bed with upper management?

Miller sat quietly in his car while Igor lay silently in his bed. I watched Miller and listened to Igor, but neither man moved. I watched for nineteen minutes until a black Mercedes sedan pulled into the parking lot. The unmarked car flashed its lights once, and the Mercedes pulled in beside it. The two cars were snug together in the adjoining spaces. They stayed like that for a few minutes, probably talking through lowered windows, until Miller squeezed out of the police car. The man in the Mercedes followed — it was Sergei Vidal.

I waited, watching the Mercedes for more bodies, but there were none. Sergei had come alone. Sergei and Miller together must have been a result of a battle of wants and needs. Sergei needed Igor dead because he believed he was turning on him. Sergei was four men down, and Miller was the only way to get to Igor right away, so he had to work with him. Sergei needed Miller. Miller wanted the money working with Sergei would offer, but more than that he wanted to live. He must have insisted that Sergei come alone. That way, no one would kill him too. Miller needed Sergei alone to get what he wanted. Wants and needs had brought them together to kill a man in Room Thirteen.

Both men walked wordlessly across the parking lot. Whatever they had to say had been said when they were parked. Miller raised a fat arm and pointed to the room next to mine. Sergei, a man in his fifties with salt and pepper hair and wearing a black turtleneck and black pants, scanned the parking lot. He saw something to his left and said something I couldn't hear, or lip read, to Miller. Sergei broke away from the other man and strode across the parking lot towards whatever he saw. As he walked, he reached inside his coat and pulled out a knife. He opened the knife and let it hang low in his left hand brushing against his thigh as he walked. The only thing in front of him would be the manager's office. I remembered the glow of the television splashing out onto the puddles on the pavement as the kid inside working nights watched Romero movies — he'd never see the Russian coming. Sergei was beefy; his chest was barrel shaped, and he walked proudly with his shoulders back. His form told me he was powerful as a young man and surely now still stronger than most. His bulky frame left my view.

I used the time the murder in the office would take to concentrate on Miller. He had taken a spot to the left of Igor's door. His fat back was so close I could have touched him from the open doorway. I took a few steps back and pulled out the .45. Sergei would know the room was occupied when he killed the manager. The info would be in the logbook. If he decided to try to do the occupant of the room like he did the manager, he would find the black eye of the .45 instead of a punk kid. If that happened, I would have to work on the fly. I backed up to the hole I had made in the drywall and listened with my eyes, and the gun, trained on the door. After a few minutes, the door inside Room Thirteen creaked open and shut.

There was silence while Miller and Sergei approached

the body. I took a few steps away from the wall, out of earshot, and powered up the phone. I got Morrison after one ring. "Escarpment Motel just up the street. Room Thirteen. Now!" I hung up the phone and put my ear back to the wall.

"Wake up, motherfucker!" Miller said.

There was a murmuring that must have started somewhere inside Igor's broken ribs.

"What's that? Speak up."

Another murmur.

"He's fucking high or something. I told you he was on the stuff. He doesn't even know where he is, but we know, don't we?"

"Finish it and let's go," Sergei said.

"Go ahead, Sergei. Do it."

"*Nyet*. You want in? This is the way. Otherwise, I will never trust you. You want to work for me? Fine. Do your first job."

"I work for money, not for free."

"Fine, fine. You will be paid, now do it."

"Well, I do like to make a good first impression. Tell ya what, Igor. I think the grief of killing your wife became too much for you to bear. You ran, got high, and then shot yourself with your own gun."

There was some grunting and rustling before Miller said, "Stand back. You don't want any brain matter on you. The spatter on the wall and ceiling has to be perfect, or someone will know there was someone standing near the body. Plus, that shit never gets out. We caught a body one time . . ."

"Do it!"

BANG.

"Take the shotgun," Sergei said.

"Is it yours?"

"You work for me now. We are not partners, so shut the fuck up and get in the car. *Da?*"

"Yeah, yeah. I mean *da, da.*"

I got away from the wall and back to the peephole. A new car was parked in the middle of the lot. Detective Sergeant Huata Morrison was walking from the car to Room Thirteen. I eased the door open a crack so I could hear what went on outside.

Morrison drew his gun and screamed "Freeze!" when he saw Sergei leave the room. In his hands was the same squat revolver he had aimed at me in the cemetery.

Sergei said nothing.

"Hands where I can see them!"

If Sergei moved, I couldn't see it.

"It's all right, Morrison. I got this handled."

"Miller?" Morrison was confused — his voice gave it away.

"Yes, sir. I've been on this Rusky for months now, and I finally got him red-handed."

"What happened here, Miller?" Morrison lowered his gun, keeping two hands on the revolver; it was a textbook safety procedure.

"Single gunshot to the face inside the room. Sergei Vidal shot and killed Igor Kerensky."

"And you caught him?"

"Yes, sir."

"How did you know he would be here?"

"CI, sir. Tipped me off an hour ago at the scene. That's why I left. I'm sorry I couldn't tell you, but these bastards have ears everywhere. There's dirty cops everywhere on the force."

"So you caught Sergei Vidal with that shotgun?" Morrison's head gestured to the gun I couldn't see from my spot behind the door.

"Yes, sir."

"That is some good police work. My only question is: why is the suspect not cuffed? Why is he free to walk with you a few feet behind?"

There was no answer, at least not in words. A bullet took the back of Morrison's skull off. The big cop stumbled back, as his body figured out what his brain could no longer tell it, and fell to the pavement.

I wasn't surprised. Morrison was in a dark parking lot with a bent cop and the head of the city's Russian muscle, and he never thought to keep his gun up. I wasn't sure if Morrison was still trying to believe Miller over me or if he had no idea how deeply corrupt Miller really was. Whatever his reasons, Morrison died with his hand on his gun. He should have seen it coming like I did through the crack in the door. I made no noise as I adapted to the situation by holstering the .45 and slipping out the Glock police pistol.

"Sorry I took so long to get out there. When I heard Morrison's voice, I went back for Igor's gun. New story is Igor killed his wife, got high, shot a cop, then turned the gun on himself. Tragic story — film at eleven."

Sergei laughed, "I think you have Russian in you."

If Miller did, the Russian in him was all over the pavement a second later.

I opened the door and pulled the trigger of the Glock. Miller caught the movement of the door, turned his head, and brought Igor's gun up. He was a second too late. Three bullets went into his chest. I pivoted to gun down Sergei, but he was already moving. Instead of going for a gun, he put his body behind Miller's staggering form and went for the shotgun still in his hand. I put a bullet in Miller's thigh, and his huge body lurched back into Sergei. The Russian gave up on the shotgun in favour of keeping the obese cop from falling on him. Sergei didn't hesitate;

MIKE KNOWLES

he used a shoulder to prop the fat man up while he went for the police pistol still on Miller's hip. The grope under the cop's cheap jacket took a few seconds as Sergei held Miller up while stretching his arm around the massive torso; it was enough time for me to shoot Miller's other leg. Sergei wasn't strong enough to hold the 300 plus pounds of dead weight up. Miller fell forward, leaving Sergei standing unarmed.

"Evening," I said.

"You were the one who came for Igor."

"Yes."

"But you do not work for him."

"No."

"Who do you work for?"

"No one anymore."

"He said someone was after him. A James Moriarty. Is that you?"

"It's who he thought I was."

"I know that name, Moriarty. It is a fake, *da?*"

"Yes."

"He was the nemesis of the detective Sherlock Holmes."

"You read the books?"

"*Pah,* books. Those books were not party approved. I learned the name when I came to Canada. I heard it on *Star Trek*. The robot fought Moriarty, the master criminal. Is this what you are, the master criminal? If so, you should come work for me. I need good criminals."

"I'm not a master criminal, I'm just one of the bad guys. The one who doesn't get caught. I don't want a job. Way I see it, you'd just string me along until you had a shot at killing me. You tried it before, and you would again."

Sergei's eyebrow rose, and he looked at me with a hawk's peering gaze. "I know you?"

"We never met, but I knew Ivan and a man named Mikhail. They were both on their way out when I met them."

Sergei's veined fists clenched the air, and he said, "I know you."

"Did the robot on *Star Trek* catch Moriarty?" I asked.

The question caused Sergei to falter. He thought about it. "*Nyet,*" he said.

"So what chance do you have?" The Glock erupted twice, and Sergei went down. I pulled the cloth from my pocket, wiped the pistol down, and put it in Morrison's dead hand. Death was everywhere, but enough of the wrong people were dead to make it a quiet case. Two cops shot and killed each other along with a mob boss and his trusted lieutenant. Morrison and Miller would be branded as corrupt, and their deaths would be whitewashed. Whatever Morrison had on me would be branded as tainted by corruption, deemed unusable, and probably destroyed or "lost" forever. The top brass would want it that way out of fear that Morrison's corruption becoming known would call into question every case he had ever worked.

I got in the Volvo and left the parking lot dialling a 911 call as I got onto the road. When the call ended, I took apart the phone and let each piece fall on a different stretch of road.

CHAPTER EIGHTEEN

O utside Sully's Tavern, I took the Colt apart and fed it to several sewer grates. The shoulder rig and belt holster went inside a garbage can chained to a light post down the street from the bar.

Inside were the same bunch of regulars I'd seen two years before in the same seats. I sat at the bar and ordered a Coke. Behind the bar, Steve filled a glass and walked it over to me.

"Still in town?" Steve spoke as though I hadn't been gone for years.

"Leaving now. I just wanted to stop by to see how you and Sandra were."

"Sandra will be sorry she missed you. With the baby on the way, she goes to bed early."

I smiled and grabbed a hold of the shaggy-haired man across the bar. We hugged, and Steve actually laughed.

"Someone was looking for you," he said.

"Who?" My neck was hot all of a sudden.

"Said she was a friend of your uncle's."

"What does she look like?"

"Small, dark hair, Asian, in her fifties. Pretty lady. Always alone."

"You sure?"

Steve's look said he was.

"She coming back?"

"Been coming 'round every couple of days for the past few weeks. She said she knew you were in town and that you would probably stop in here. Guess she was right."

"When was she last in?"

"Two nights ago."

I wanted to know what Ruby Chu wanted, and I had no reason to run anymore. Everyone who wanted me dead was cold. I had no illusions that Death would learn my name eventually, but he could get in line when the time came. I stayed on the bar stool for a few hours, then I went looking for the woman who knew my uncle to find out what she wanted with me.

MIKE KNOWLES